Mission for the Maharaja

A Patricia Fisher Mystery

Book 7

Steve Higgs

Dedication

To all the people out there pursuing a career as a storyteller.

Table of Contents:

Author Note:

Extract from A Sleuth and her Dachshund in Athens

Dead Relative

A New Mystery to Solve

Private Jet

I was almost asleep when Barbie's voice brought me back to the present. 'I could get used to this,' she said. Across the cabin from me, Barbie was receiving a massage; a female masseuse going tito town on her shoulders while I luxuriated in the afterglow of my own head to toe treatment.

That the Maharaja's personal jet had a spa on board should give you some indication of just how impressively opulent it was. Now, consider that I am currently the guest staying in the royal suite on board the world's most luxurious cruise liner and then think about what it would take to impress me. Trust me, this aircraft was a whole new level. The captain had taken immense pride in welcoming us on board himself, then invited each of us to visit the cockpit because, unlike commercial flights, they didn't have to lock themselves in for fear of being hijacked. The plane was manufactured by Bombardier Business Aircraft and was their top of the range Global 8000 with a number of additional extras, the captain assured us. I wasn't sure what all the extras were but there were eight of us on board and so far I had counted more than twenty staff including the pilot and co-pilot.

Rick and Akamu had gone straight to the bar where they had ordered Jack and coke from the stunningly pretty barmaid there. All of the staff were stunningly pretty for that matter, chosen for their looks, unless everyone in Zangrabar was equally beautiful.

The hosts in the cabin were led by Omar, a handsome man in his early forties. His clipped beard and close-cropped hair were dotted with flecks of grey, but it just made him more attractive to my mind. He explained the aircraft in more detail once we were in the air, stating that the Maharaja had a small fleet of the aircraft and changed them each year. Of course, it was a new Maharaja now that the old one had so recently died.

1

He talked about the bar and kitchen, explaining that the flight would take a little more than four hours and the crew were here to ensure that our every wish was fulfilled. When he got to the bit about the spa, Barbie's head had snapped around, and her hand went up to ask a question.

Omar smiled widely at her. 'Miss Berkeley there is no need to raise your hand. We are your servants. Just click your finger if you so desire.'

'Goodness I would never,' she said, sounding horrified by the idea. 'Sorry, did I just hear you say the word spa?'

He gave his broad smile again and a dip of his head. 'Yes, Miss Berkeley. If you would like to follow Amia,' he indicated a member of crew standing a few feet to his left, 'she will be happy to escort you to the spa when you are ready.' Barbie was out of her seat like it had given her an electric shock. She paused to kiss Hideki on his forehead, then grabbed Deepa's arm and yanked her out of her chair.

Barbie's Pakistani friend said something that sounded like, 'Urk,' as Barbie made her jump and she dropped the magazine she had been reading. Deepa Bhukari and Martin Baker (I had finally learned his first name) were along as security at Alistair's request. I was happy to have them with me though; I liked them both and Deepa was probably Barbie's best friend if one didn't count Jermaine. For the next few days, they were essentially off duty and having a holiday; I suspected some jealousy arose among their colleagues that these two got to come away with me. Before we left the ship, I insisted they leave their uniforms behind and now they both looked like completely different people in their civilian attire. Deepa especially since she was wearing flattering clothes for the first time in my company, plus makeup, and her hair wasn't pulled into a tight bun for once. Instead, it flowed over one shoulder in a cascade of beautiful, black waves. She was really quite attractive.

'Come on, ladies,' called Barbie, starting to drag Deepa toward the back of the aircraft. 'It's time to get pampered.'

And pamper time it was. The chaps did not seem inclined to join us which suited us just fine, so I plopped my rather-surprised-to-be-awake-looking Dachshund on Rick's lap at the bar and followed the other ladies. And there we were in the spa, getting massaged and having our toenails painted and generally feeling like the luckiest people on earth.

But this is me we are talking about: Patricia the disaster magnet. So the wonderful fog of exotic botanicals I had lost myself in went sideways as the aircraft jinked hard to the right. Then a sudden, and very unwelcome sensation of weightlessness occurred as the aircraft dropped out from beneath me and I hung in the air for a half second. I locked eyes with Barbie, as she too, floated for a heartbeat, then we both crashed back down onto our beds and the panic started.

The ladies working in the spa clearly had no idea what was happening either, the terror on their faces doing nothing to help my evaporating calm. Then a voice boomed over the tannoy, 'Get everyone into a seat and strap them in!' Fear for my own safety melted away when I heard Anna bark. She was in the next room as I had left her in Rick's care and though I was certain he would do his best for her, our aircraft appeared to be in trouble.

The plane was taking evasive manoeuvres, or that was how it seemed. It pitched to the left as I threw myself off the massage table, the combination of changing forces and gravity tossing me into Barbie as she tried to get to her feet. We had on towels and nothing else, Deepa Bhukari doing slightly better on the clothing front because she opted for a head massage and pedicure. I needed both hands to hold on to whatever I could grab for balance and another hand just to hold up the damned towel.

The panic-stricken masseuses tried to guide us back through the door out of the spa so we could find our seats but looked ready to abandon us to save themselves. Mercifully, Omar arrived in the doorway to grab Barbie's hand and get her to safety. Somehow, her towel was wrapped tightly around her body and staying up: she might as well have been wearing a dress.

Deepa clambered over a massage table and followed the last masseuse out the door leaving just me in the spa, clinging to a chair and bracing myself against the wall. Pressing my back to the wall was the only thing keeping my towel up. I needed to unwrap it and start again but that required two hands which I didn't have.

Omar's face appeared in the doorway again. Urgent gestures accompanied by a shout to get me moving. 'Mrs Fisher! I have to get you somewhere safer than this.'

To accentuate his point, the pilot spun the aircraft and took it into a dive. I held on for dear life, but as he brought it back to level, I accepted defeat and ran for the door, trying to grab the towel as it betrayed me and stayed where it was. I snagged one corner of it and ran with it behind me like it was a kite or a flag. Omar's eyes went wide as I gave him a look at everything I had to show, my boobs bouncing uncomfortably in every direction until I fell into his arms and he helped me into a seat.

'What is happening?' I shouted over the noise of the engines. They were roaring as the pilot pushed them.

Omar shoved me into a chair and yanked a belt into place to hold me down. 'We're under attack,' he yelled back, then decided I was safe enough and dived into a chair of his own.

We were under attack? Why the heck were we under attack? I glanced out of the window next to me and caught a glimpse of the land beneath

4

us; we were much lower than we had been and much lower than I expected unless we were coming in to land, which we very much were not.

'Hold on please, ladies and gentlemen,' the voice was the captain's and he managed to sound calm, but the instruction preceded him barrel-rolling the aircraft and getting even closer to the ground. He was hugging the landscape now, evading whoever or whatever it was that was supposedly attacking us. We had been in the air for little more than an hour so were nowhere near Zangrabar yet and I really didn't know what country might be beneath us right now. Not that geography would matter much if we crashed.

I pulled the treacherous towel so that it covered as much of me as possible and looked about the cabin at my friends. They were all strapped into their chairs and looked like they were all saying personal prayers of some kind. Hideki was looking at Barbie, the two of them separated by twenty yards or more. Rick and Akamu had moved from the bar but had taken their drinks with them. Rick kept trying to have a sip of his, but the aircraft wouldn't stay still long enough so it slopped each time he got it near his lips. I heard him mutter some rude words. Then Anna popped her head up to look at me. She was tucked under Rick's arm and appeared to be clinging to him. If Dachshunds have a worried expression, it was the one she was currently wearing.

Deepa had found a seat next to Martin Baker and the two of them were holding hands. I couldn't tell if that was a camaraderie thing, or just the desire to feel connected to someone at the end. I didn't want it to be the end though, I wanted the captain to find a way to escape the threat pursuing us. Just as I said that silent prayer though, we all heard the sound of something hitting the aircraft. Something that sounded very much like bullets.

An alarm started wailing in the cockpit, another sound to add to the confusion and terror. Then I caught sight of something as I glanced out of the window again; a small aircraft, what looked like a fighter plane, had come along side us. Then another appeared. I couldn't see what flag they were flying but a whoop of joy from the cockpit stopped my anxiety from bubbling over.

'Ladies and gentlemen,' the pilot said as he evened out the aircraft, throttled back and began to rise into the sky again. 'I think the danger is passed. We have an escort from our allies in the United Republic of Zarrania.'

All around me, the crew of the aircraft were looking relieved and starting to unbuckle themselves from their seats. I felt no such relief. All I felt was anxious that the danger might not have truly passed. Beyond that, I really, really wanted to know why someone had attacked us.

'Hey there's a hole in wing!' shouted Akamu, causing Rick to join him in staring out of the window on his side of the plane. Crew rushed over to see as well and both Baker and Bhukari left their seats to see the damage. With all the attention focused in the other direction, I slipped from my seat and back into the spa area to find my clothes. I had been naked for quite long enough, thank you.

A few minutes later and my pulse was returning to a normal speed as I tied the thin belt back around my waist and slipped on my low-heeled shoes. At least now if we crashed, they would find my remains fully clothed. Barbie's pile of clothing was where she had left it, albeit less neatly stacked than it had been due to the mid-air acrobatics. No doubt she was still happily wandering around in her towel.

She wasn't wandering around though; when I left the spa, I found her sitting at the bar with Rick, Akamu, and everyone else. There was a spare seat next to her with an unattended cold gin and tonic parked in front of it. She saw the barman flick his eyes in my direction and turned to see me approach. 'Hey, Patty. I figured you might want a drink.'

'You figured right,' I said as I sat down and grabbed the glass with both hands. 'How's everyone doing?'

I got a chorus of, 'Better nows,' and, 'Be glad to get on the grounds,' from everyone.

Rick said, 'Are you okay, Patricia? You looked like you got thrown around a bit there.' I felt my face radiating heat as I remembered jiggling my way into my seat with my towel trailing behind me. 'Not that anyone saw anything,' he added quickly, taking particular interest in his glass instead of looking at me.

I took a swig of my gin and tonic, opened my mouth to speak but the sweeping hit of ice-cold botanicals gripped me, and I downed the rest of the glass in a single hit.

'Wow,' said Barbie. 'I guess you needed that.'

'Is the pilot looking for somewhere to land?' I asked.

Just then, his voice boomed over the tannoy again. 'Ladies and gentlemen, you undoubtedly have some questions about what just happened. I'm afraid at this time I don't have many answers for you. This aircraft is fitted with radar detection equipment, so we were able to identify that we were about to be attacked and take evasive action. I apologise that I didn't have enough time to give a warning. There is some minor damage to the portside wing, but I believe we are safe to continue to our original destination in Zangrabar City. The nearest airport we could divert to is only a few miles closer and we have a military escort now, so whoever attacked us will not be back.' He sounded certain that the

7

danger was over though I didn't share his confidence. 'We have approximately two hours flight time left, so sit back, please relax and be assured that we will land safely in Zangrabar in due course.'

As I nodded to the barman to bring me another gin and tonic, I wondered who had attacked us and why. I had been off the ship for just a couple of hours and I was already in trouble.

It would be a while before I found out just how deep that trouble went.

Reception

The rest of the flight passed without incident and I had actually managed to relax by the time the crew opened the door and welcomed us to Zangrabar. The cool air-conditioned air in the cabin was replaced by a blast from a furnace as I approached the blinding sunshine coming through the door. The air outside was dry and intensely hot; heat haze creating a shimmer in the air as I looked across the runway.

At the bottom of the stairs was a red carpet, which to one side had a band which burst into tune the moment I poked my head out of the door. To the other side was a small fleet of shining black Rolls Royces. Just before them, and essentially blocking our way was a man in an ornate military uniform, rows of medals adorning both sides of his chest. Just behind him was a man in what my brain told me was traditional Zangrabarian garb, which is to say that he looked like Aladdin and had a turban on his head. He could be the Maharaja for all I knew, and it suddenly occurred to me that I hadn't thought to look the man up. A simple internet search would have provided me with pictures and some background. There just hadn't been time, I guess. Just behind the pair of them was a man in a sharp, grey, business suit.

I descended the stairs with Jermaine in my shadow and everyone else following. Below me, a sea of smiles looked up, tracking my progress. I kept one hand on the railing because this was the perfect time for a Patricia moment where I fell down the stairs in front of royalty, most likely landing knickers side up with my dress around my ears.

The man in uniform stepped forward as I reached the bottom step, then bent from the waist in an ornate bow. Oh, cripes, what was I expected to do now? The man in the sharp suit and the man my brain labelled as Aladdin also bowed, getting their torsos lower than their waists as they did.

9

Feeling awkward, I returned the bow, hoping that was the right thing to do. Behind me, I heard the others shuffling their feet and doing as I had, Akamu groaning as he tried to bend.

'Your Eminence. It is my most grateful honour to welcome you to Zangrabar on behalf of his excellency the Maharaja.' He was having to shout to be heard above the sound of the band. I risked a peek to see that the three people sent to greet us were standing again. I straightened myself, then hissed at my companions. There was more groaning as my elder companions got themselves back to upright.

'I hope those cars are air-conditioned,' muttered Rick, echoing what I was already thinking. A trickle of perspiration ran down my back.

The band reached a crescendo and finally stopped, the conductor performing an abrupt about turn to face me and then bowed deeply from the waist just like everyone else. This time, I just gave him a smile and a wave.

The soldier came forward with a warm smile. 'Mrs Fisher, honoured guests, the Maharaja is awaiting your arrival with much excitement. He asked me to express his disappointment that he could not be here to greet you in person. Preparations for his coronation in two days' time have demanded his presence at the palace.' He gestured to the two men behind him, stepping to his right so we could see them. 'This is Osama Al-Kaisi, the administrator for the palace. Every element of your stay in Zangrabar is his responsibility.'

He spoke for the first time, 'If you need anything during your stay, you need only ask. Each of you will be assigned a personal valet to attend to your needs.'

Rick's voice interrupted him, 'Hey, that sounds good.'

He smiled in Rick's direction and bowed his head gracefully. 'Your wish will be our command, sir.'

Then the soldier switched his attention to the man that looked like Aladdin. 'Your Eminence, this is Aladdin Alshaibi.' I smirked at his name despite myself and had to force the mirth from my face before someone saw it. 'He is your personal valet and has been appointed to you by the Maharaja himself.'

I smiled at Aladdin. 'I'm very pleased to meet you.'

Just behind me, Jermaine spluttered. 'Say what, now? I am Mrs Fisher's personal butler. Providing for her is my duty.'

With a smile still in place, Aladdin bowed deeply as he replied, 'Not in Zangrabar, sir. Here you are our honoured guest and will be treated as if you were visiting royalty. That is my instruction from the Maharaja.'

Jermaine did not look happy. I brought his attention to look at me and I pinched his right cheek between my thumb and forefinger as I laughed at him. 'It sounds terrible, doesn't it? You'll just have to find a way to put up with it, Jermaine dear.'

Yet again, Aladdin bowed so deeply I worried he might overbalance. 'The honour is entirely ours, Eminence.' I had just about got used to being called madam every two minutes. I knew it would be a waste of my time to argue with them or insist they all call me Patricia instead, but Eminence seemed a bit much.

The soldier then finally introduced himself. 'I am General Aziz, head of the Zangrabrian Joint Forces.' He gave yet another sweeping bow.

'Are we in danger?' I asked, voicing a concern I was sure every one of my friends shared. 'We almost got shot down just getting here.'

The general bowed his head as if ashamed. 'May I offer my most sincere apologies for the scare you must have suffered. Zangrabar is a mineral rich country and we are not without enemies. I had not anticipated that your flight might be targeted and for that, I am truly sorry.'

I waved off his apology. 'General, we arrived alive. If you could get us back to the ship in one piece three days from now, that would be great. Until then, I assume we are safe here in Zangrabar?'

He bowed deeply yet again. 'Your Eminence, Mrs Fisher. I give you my personal guarantee. I will be honoured to sacrifice my life to protect yours.'

I grimaced at the thought. 'Let's hope that isn't necessary.'

Moving off the subject of death, the general swept an arm toward the line of cars. 'It is warm out today. Perhaps we should make our way to the palace.' His suggestion was met with a general round of approval from my friends, the most vocal of which, Rick, had something to say.

'I sure hope these fancy cars have a stocked bar on board.'

The general's response brought him up short. 'Oh, no, sir. Zangrabar is an alcohol-free country.'

Rick spun around to stare at him. 'I sure hope you mean that alcohol is free in Zangrabar and not that other thing.'

General Aziz was full of smiles for the foolish American. 'I'm terribly sorry, sir. Alcohol was outlawed here more than sixty years ago. Unlike America's problems in the 1920s, prohibition works very well here, creating a healthy, sober society. There is very little crime associated with alcohol, its consumption, illegal sale or distribution.'

My entire party had stopped halfway to the cars. Rick was looking longingly back at the plane, possibly wondering if he could wait there for us because he knew the bar to be stocked. I had to admit I felt a pang of loss and some concern about gin separation anxiety over the next few days.

Barbie shrugged though. 'I bet they have a great gym at the palace. We can all get in some exercise and feel great when we get back to the ship.' She said it with such enthusiasm, truly looking forward to it most likely. The grumbling responses from everyone else did little to dent the bounce in her step as she dragged Hideki toward the nearest Rolls Royce. 'Come on, sweetie,' she laughed. 'I've never been in a Rolls.'

Her spirit buoyed everyone else's as we piled into the cars, a dutiful valet standing ready to open the doors on each car except the one I was heading for. Jermaine darted forward to get the handle, but Aladdin rushed around him to get the door first, bowing low as he opened it for me. 'Your Eminence, Mrs Fisher.' I thought Jermaine was going to growl or slap the man's hand away from the handle, but he managed to contain himself, settling for a scowl instead.

Barbie and Hideki were already in their car, likewise Rick and Akamu. The doors of the car in front of mine closed, signalling Martin and Deepa were also aboard and ready to go. With another shove, I managed to get Jermaine into our car and finally the door could close. Mercifully, the air inside was cooler than outside despite the door being open for so long. No sooner were we in our seats than the cavalcade began moving. Jermaine and I were sitting on the back seat facing forwards, Aladdin sitting opposite us and facing rearwards. He was already beginning to prepare drinks – non-alcoholic ones and had a fancy brass coffee pot with a very long spout.

On our way to the palace, Aladdin served us thin, sweet pastries filled with pistachios and dates and hot apple tea, a traditional afternoon snack, he assured me. While we ate, he told us about his country, its rich history and traditions and the part it played in the global economy. He also told us about a banquet the Maharaja wished to hold in my honour this evening.

The news surprised me. I wasn't sure I wanted a banquet in my honour; I'm just a cleaning lady from England. Who am I to be honoured by a Maharaja? When I said that though, Aladdin told me the sapphire was said to contain magical powers that ensured the future prosperity of the nation and of the throne. Its return had been the subject of great jubilation and partying across the whole nation. A banquet in my honour was the very least the Maharaja could do. I accepted that it was going to happen, I saw no way of avoiding it now I was here. It wasn't as if I could say, "No thanks," now was it?

Our journey was a short one; less than thirty minutes from the airport to the palace which began to loom in the windscreen long before we arrived. It was a seriously impressive structure; eight tall towers with bulbous tops reaching into the sky marked the periphery and a high wall spanned between them all. Inside, a massive and ornate structure with yet more towers dominated.

The cars swept up a long, two-lane driveway and through a wide gate in the outer wall. Where everything outside was desert and occasional palm trees, inside the walls, it was lush green grass, clipped bushes with bright flowers and ornate lakes. It was quite beautiful.

Through the windscreen, I could see another reception party waiting for us. It was far more grand than the one at the airport and was flanked by twelve riders on elephants. The over-the-topness continued as the cars came to a halt in a line and a fanfare erupted from dozens of long trumpets.

More valets dashed forward to get our doors and a fresh blast of hot, dry, desert air smacked me in the face before I could get out. As I clambered from the car, I picked Anna up and tucked her under my left arm. I had no idea what the punishment for biting a Maharaja might be, but I doubted it would be a supply of gravy bones. A small man exited the palace doors right in front of me, emerging from the shadows being carried on a round bed of cushions by a dozen men. Two more men held huge, ornate shades over his head. They were in the shape of palm fronds.

Had there been any doubt in my mind that I was looking at the Maharaja, I would have known for certain when the elephants bowed. I didn't bow, Aladdin assured me in the car it was not expected of my party; we were considered by the Maharaja to be his equals. I would do my best to uphold that but wondered what he might make of Rick and Akamu.

'It's so pretty,' whispered Barbie, coming to stand next to me. 'I feel like I fell into a story book.' I knew what she meant; if I found a flying carpet in my room, I was not going to be the slightest bit surprised.

I heard Deepa say, 'I bet he's handsome. He sure is rich. Maybe he would consider a woman from Pakistan as a bride. I could get used to living here.'

To my other side, Rick said, 'Is it me or is the Maharaja a little on the little side?' I was thinking the same thing, but I wasn't going to say it out loud. As he came closer though, I realised that he wasn't small, or at least he wasn't a small man, he just wasn't fully grown yet; he was a boy.

Deepa said, 'Ah, nuts.'

The bed carriers stopped walking, neatly coming to a stop in unison before lowering the Maharaja to the ground. Then the young man unfolded from his three-quarter prone position and stepped off the bed of cushions.

All around me, all those that had been bowing, now stood up again. The Maharaja was looking at me, his hands folded neatly behind his back as he advanced. Like the other men, he wore a turban, though his appeared to be studded with diamonds and other precious jewels that glinted in the sun.

As he came forward, I handed Anna to Jermaine so my hands were free to greet him. The Maharaja unfolded his arms and I believed he meant to offer me his hand to shake. I was right, but only sort of. As the unelected leader of our little group, I offered my hand to grasp his and said, 'Good afternoon, Your Majesty, thank you so much for inviting us to your beautiful home.'

'Hey, no problem, babe,' he replied in an American accent while gripping my thumb in an overhand handshake then, letting go, backhanding it with the same hand and then proceeding to grip my fingertips with his. I stared at our hands in bewilderment as he used his other hand to help form my hand into complicated shapes to complete his ornate handshake. 'What's happening? Nice touch sending back the sapphire, that thing is da'bomb!'

I was literally dumbstruck. I had no idea what was happening, but Barbie asked the question at the front of the queue in my head. 'You sound like you're from California?'

He swung his head in her direction, paused, looked her up and down and concluded with, 'Hubba hubba. Girl you fill that dress like a dream I had last night.'

Barbie's mouth dropped open. 'Excuse me?'

'I ain't never had me a blonde girl. Vizier!' he shouted over his shoulder and a grey-haired gentleman with a long beard shuffled out from the crowd of onlookers.

He wore ornate robes that came all the way to his feet and held a long staff in his right hand, the top of which was shaped to resemble a cobra. 'Your Excellence?'

'Why are there no white women in my harem?' the boy Maharaja snapped. He sounded angry.

Keeping his tone calm and patient, the elder man replied, 'Because you have not requested them, Your Majesty.'

'Well, now I am.' He paused as if waiting for something, then, when the old man didn't move away, he flapped an arm at him. 'That will be all, Vizier.' All I could do was stare at the rude boy. This wasn't what I had expected at all. 'Sorry about him,' the Maharaja said. 'Good help is so hard to find. No doubt you are all tired from your journey. I understand you ran into some trouble on your way. Please make yourself at home in my palace, I believe you will find it comfortable. I have other duties to attend to, but I hope to see you all this evening for a feast in your honour.'

This was a little better; he had dropped the vulgar attitude and was playing at being host. I was utterly confused about why he sounded like his next word was going to be, 'Dude,' but maybe I would get answers once we were inside. No doubt Aladdin could explain the incongruity.

The Maharaja walked back to his bed and was once again lifted into the air by the burly men as they carried him back inside the shade of the palace. As he departed, the Vizier came forward again, taking over

17

procedures to disperse the attending crowd. 'Please follow me,' he requested. 'Your bags and belongings will follow.'

I glanced back at the cars to see a line of men carrying our bags. Jermaine still looked a little lost now that he had nothing to do so I took his hand and pulled him after me. 'Come along, Jermaine. You're just going to have to relax. Maybe they will have a pool so you can go swimming.'

Rick clapped him on the arm as he past. 'You can do anything you want here, buddy, just as long as you don't want a drink.' I grimaced as his comment was overheard, but none of our hosts saw fit to respond as the eight of us, led by the vizier with his elegant staff, and followed by an entire entourage of helpers, followed the Maharaja's floating bed back inside the palace.

The oppressive heat outside faded the moment we gained the shade. I breathed a sigh of relief but tapped Aladdin on his shoulder. He spun around to face me and bowed. 'Yes, Your Eminence?'

'Is it always this hot here?' I asked while fanning myself. Among my friends I seemed to be the only one really affected by it. Rick and Akamu were from Hawaii, a tropical island paradise, Jermaine hailed from Jamaica, Barbie from California, Bhukari from Pakistan— all far hotter climates than the rather drizzly corner of England where I had spent my life. Martin came from Northern Ireland, an even drizzlier place than England but had been on board the Aurelia and other cruise ships for many years now so was acclimated.

Aladdin's face looked concerned as if perhaps his esteemed guest was demanding he do something about the weather. 'Oh, no, Your Eminence, today it is unseasonably cool. There are concerns that it might spoil the coronation.'

He thought it was cool today, that was just what I wanted to hear. I continued to waft air into my face, but it was far cooler inside the palace and I soon stopped, not because I had cooled down though, but because I was staring in awe at the building I was being led through. The cool temperature was achieved not through air-conditioning but by using half the world's supply of marble. It was everywhere. The bits that weren't marble appeared to be gold and there was a lot of gold.

'Still think he's too young?' Barbie teased Deepa.

Deepa gave her friend a set of very wide eyes and shrugged that she might have changed her mind: this was money on a hitherto undreamt of scale. The corridors and passageways were wide expanses that an average house would fit into sideways and the ceilings had to be four metres above my head. Every window we passed revealed a fountain or some ornate sculpture beyond it in the fantastic gardens outside.

Then we came into a wider expanse, the room spreading out on either side of us, but a raised platform in the centre of the room was what drew everyone's attention.

'Oh my, life,' gasped Akamu. 'Is that it?'

Rick snapped his head around to stare at me. 'I know you said it was big, Patricia, but...' He couldn't find the words to finish the sentence as everyone else spread out to get a good look and he wandered away with them.

On a raised plinth on top of the platform was the sapphire of Zangrabar. A glass dome covered it and I could see complex security systems set into the ceiling – anti-theft devices no doubt. I had to admit that it was a big jewel; bigger than both my fists clamped together.

A shaft of light coming from directly above the jewel filled it with radiant light which created patterns like a kaleidoscope on every surface in the room. It was quite magical.

The vizier paused to let my group look at it. I think only Lieutenant Baker had seen it before, when it was first recovered aboard the Aurelia. 'Prosperity and good fortune will return to this land now that we have the jewel back,' the vizier said proudly.

Rick whistled in appreciation, but it was time to move on. Anna was tugging at her lead to get somewhere even though she had no idea where she was or where she might be going. With his staff clomping on the floor with every other step, the vizier continued to lead us through the immense palace until he declared that we had reached the guest quarters. 'Many nation's dignitaries are already here, though many more are yet to arrive. There is a suite and a personal valet on hand for each of you. If there is anything you desire, you need only ask for it.'

I heard Rick mutter something about a Jack and coke under his breath but if the vizier heard, he paid him no attention. At the mention of valets, eight men appeared in the passageway, each coming out of a different room. The doors stretched away into the distance though, each of them fifty feet apart.

'I'll take the first one,' volunteered Rick. 'I need to get off these feet.'

'I might as well have the next then,' said Akamu, shuffling onwards as Rick peeled off to go into his room. We didn't get very far before we heard an expletive echo back out from Rick's room. It wasn't uttered in panic or shock though; it was the sound of awe.

Rick staggered back out into the passageway behind us. 'Guys, my room's bigger than the ship. I can't even see to the other end.'

The vizier smiled. 'Each of you is staying in one of our staterooms. Alongside you will be royalty from other nations and visiting heads of state. Queen Elizabeth is due to arrive tomorrow morning.'

Barbie's jaw almost hit the marble floor. 'The Queen?'

'Yes,' the vizier replied with another smile.

'The Queen of England is coming here?'

'Yes.'

'To stay in this palace at the same time as me?'

'Yes.'

Barbie grabbed Hideki's hand and started running to the next stateroom door. 'Oh. My. God! I have to get on Facebook right now!' I laughed at her, but Deepa, Jermaine and Martin echoed her sentiment and were already getting their phones out as they hurried along the passageway.

'Must be a young person thing,' said Rick, heading back into his stateroom with a shrug. His voice echoed back out, 'If anyone wants me, I'll be doing laps in my bath.'

I looked down at Anna, who looked back up at me. Her expression was hard to read, but I think she was mostly trying to impart the need for me to feed her.

'What sort of dog is that?' asked the vizier. With everyone else gone I could claim that he and I were alone in the passageway now. We weren't though, there was still a dozen or more servants, bringing cases to the staterooms, passing behind me as they followed my friends to deliver their belongings.

Anna licked her lips and yawned. 'She's a miniature Dachshund. I came by her during a visit to Japan just a short while ago.'

'Is she a Japanese dog?' The vizier was eyeing her with great curiosity.

'No. It's a German breed originally.'

'Is it an obedient breed?'

We started walking again. I was looking forward to seeing just how impressive the rooms were and what sort of view I might have. I also quite fancied a bath and the opportunity to see if I had picked up any bruises when I got thrown about on the plane. His question deserved an honest answer though, so I said, 'I think so. In general. This one, not so much. We are working on it, aren't we, little girl?'

I got no answer from Anna and a single raised eyebrow from the vizier. I guess people in Zangrabar don't talk to their dogs so much. Since we were talking, I decided it might be acceptable to ask about the Maharaja. 'The... um. The Maharaja has an unusual accent for Zangrabar, does he not?'

Carefully, the vizier smiled at me. 'He spent the last year at a school in Orange County in California. A while back he watched a television program called... I think it was *The OC*?' He clearly wasn't sure, and I couldn't comment either way. 'Then he insisted he be allowed to perfect his English in an American school and his father arranged for him to travel. He returned only when the news of the sapphire was announced and his father insisted he return.'

'His father died right after that, didn't he?'

'That is correct, Your Eminence.' We had reached the last room in the line and Aladdin was waiting patiently for me. My bags were already inside. 'Will there be anything else, Your Eminence?'

I did have another question. 'Vizier... do I address you as vizier? It sounds odd to do so.'

'I have been the vizier here for so long I barely even remember my birth name. For simplicity, everyone calls me vizier. It is both my title and my name.'

'Well, I have a question: In the Maharaja's telegram, he suggested that he had a mystery or some such for me to look into for him personally. I didn't feel like I could ask him outright but if I am not to see him until this evening at the banquet and the coronation is tomorrow, I fear I may not have sufficient time to investigate before I leave. Do you know anything about it?'

The vizier looked worried for a second. 'The Maharaja asked you to look into something for him?

'Yes.'

'But you don't know what it is?'

'Not yet.'

'I must confess that I do not know either which means that I am failing in my job. I will ask him forthwith. Please do not fret though, Your Eminence. I am sure the matter can be dealt with by my own staff, whatever it is.'

Then he turned and began walking away. He didn't say goodbye or wish me a good evening, he just started back the way we had come as if distracted suddenly. I watched him go, his staff striking the marble tile with a light thump every other step.

Now that he had left, with the exception of Aladdin, I was the only one in the passageway. Anna gave the lead a quick tug to remind me she was there. I glanced down. 'Let's get you some dinner, shall we?' Clearly the idea resonated with her as she instantly ran into the suite, zipping around Aladdin's legs and only stopping when she got to the end of her lead.

I followed her inside the vast and opulent suite, its high ceiling and wide lobby only hinting at what lay beyond. I didn't get the chance to look at it though; Aladdin grabbed my arm the moment the door was closed.

'What the heck?' I snapped as I yanked it away again. I had no idea what his intentions were, but he was about to get a face full of demented Dachshund if I let Anna's lead go. When I rounded on him though, I could see the innocent panic on his face.

'Your Eminence, I mean you no harm. Please excuse me for touching you.' His head was bowed to stare at the ground, and he looked utterly horrified as he bent his face up to look at me.

'Why did you touch me?'

'I heard what you said to the vizier: that the Maharaja contacted you about helping him solve a mystery. You are already famous here for returning the sapphire, the nation's greatest treasure, so I hope that I may turn to you in the nation's greatest moment of need.' He was still bowing his head and looking terrified as if I might summon the guards and demand his execution.

'What moment of need? What are you talking about?' Anna tugged at the lead again. 'I need to find my dog some food. Do you know where my bags have been put?' I was suddenly annoyed about my day. Someone tried to shoot down the plane I was on, the Maharaja, who I had imagined to be a perfect gentleman who would be the most amazing host, was actually a teenage boy with a raging libido, and now I was being confused by my new valet who wanted me to believe there was something terrible happening here. Irrationally or not, I was angry and was trying to distract myself by feeding Anna so it didn't bubble over in Aladdin's direction.

I left him in the lobby and went searching for my bags. Anna's bowls, bed, toys, treats, bedtime biscuits and pouches of nutritionally balanced dog food had all been packed by Jermaine and I was starting to miss the comfort of his presence. He didn't bring me problems, he brought me solutions. Every time.

I found my bags in the master bedroom. They were empty though, a quick search revealing that my clothes had been hung in wardrobes or placed into drawers. My toiletries were arranged neatly in the en suite bathroom but there was no sign of Anna's items.

'Here, Your Eminence,' called Aladdin, making himself useful and finding it for me.

'You need to stop calling me that. You can call me Mrs Fisher or madam.' I had no desire to be addressed as madam, but Jermaine insisted, and I had got used to it over the last almost two months. I would ask him to call me Patricia or even Patty like Barbie does, but I knew it would be a wasted request.

I heard Aladdin make a noise of discomfort and stopped to look at him properly for the first time. Seeing the emotion in his face, I gave in, my shoulders slumping as I accepted that I was going to get involved despite an intense desire not to. In his hands he held Anna's bed and in it were all her other things.

'She needs water in the silver bowl, and I need the bed placed next to mine.' Obediently, he started to move across the room to put her bed down. 'Then you can tell me what it is that has you so concerned.'

He flicked a glance at me and started talking immediately. 'I don't know what is happening, but the Maharaja that you met today isn't the real Maharaja.' He looked guilty saying it, like he was betraying someone in doing so, but he also looked like he believed what he was saying.

Nevertheless, his reply hit me like an uppercut. 'Not the Maharaja?' I was stunned at the suggestion, instantly wanting to scoff but stopping myself because... well, what made him assert such a concept unless he had a good reason. 'Why do you think that?' I asked.

It was then that I saw just how terrified he was about revealing his belief. He let go of a breath that he must have been holding since he first spoke and looked ready to collapse from relief that I hadn't called for security to take him away.

Anna barked her impatience, making me jump but breaking the tension in the room. I looked down at her, getting a tail wag in response: She wanted her dinner and was getting bored with the standard of service from her appointed human. I looked back up at Aladdin. 'I'm going to feed my dog. You can talk while I am doing it. I want to know why you think the Maharaja I met is... what? A double? And I want to know why you think it is a good idea to tell me of all people.' My annoyance had risen to the surface again and shown itself despite my attempts to keep calm.

'Your Emin...' he stopped and started again when I shot him a hard look. 'Mrs Fisher.' I nodded. 'Mrs Fisher, I was the personal valet of the Maharaja from the moment he was born until six days ago. I know him better than his father did. Overnight, I was reassigned to prepare for your

26

arrival. That may seem entirely innocent, but I know the Maharaja; he would never want to be without me.'

I bit my lip and shook my head. 'That's not a reason to believe the Maharaja has been replaced by a double.'

Aladdin nodded. 'That's entirely right. His voice is different and many of his mannerisms have changed. It's all subtle things that perhaps no one other than me would notice. I don't know who he is, but the boy pretending to be the Maharaja is a fake.'

I screwed my face up in disbelief. 'I think you should leave, Aladdin.' When he didn't move, I added, 'Now, please.'

Once again, he looked panic stricken. I felt bad for him, but I also felt betrayed that I was having to deal with his issues. So far as I could see, this was nothing more than Aladdin lashing out or trying to cause trouble because he had lost a coveted position. Why he had lost his job as valet to the Maharaja was a more interesting question, but it could have so many answers and be as innocent as the Maharaja recognised the need for someone new as he took the throne.

Looking ashamed, Aladdin bowed as deeply as he had at any point today and backed out of my room without another word.

I sighed deeply and leaned on the wall. This was not the deeply relaxing, incredible, once-in-a-lifetime event I expected. I left Alistair behind to come here, for goodness sake. I didn't have time to dwell on what hadn't gone right though, there was a banquet in my honour in just a few hours with a stack of guests from around the world. I had felt queasy about it before, now I just felt sick.

Finding the sapphire had been more accident than deduction. Sure, I had worked it out, but only by a process of elimination. All the praise and

27

worship and accolades they were throwing at me just made me feel uncomfortable. When the Maharaja's telegram arrived, I had felt flattered. Now though, I wish I had been wise enough to say no.

Anna barked, making me jump again. I still hadn't fed her.

Ninety minutes later, I was wondering what to do with my hair. I needed something that would work with my outfit; one which had been supplied for me especially for the banquet and was, the tailor assured me when he and his team arrived just before I got in the bath, a traditional Zangrabarian celebration outfit. I called Barbie to find that she had one too, so I wasn't being tricked into wearing it so I would look like a complete fool. I brought my own clothes with me, expecting to wear them tonight, but now, when I spilled soup down myself, it wouldn't be my clothes I ruined. Barbie told me the chaps had outfits as well, and that Hideki looked very handsome in his. I had taken the last stateroom in line, so the tailor got to me last and everyone else was already trying theirs on.

The stateroom was large and luxurious, so once the tailor and his team departed and I was utterly alone in it, I had taken my time and run a deep bath. Rick had been exaggerating about being able to do laps in it, but it was big. Certainly it was the biggest bath I had ever been in, but primping and preening and getting myself ready hadn't dispelled the sense of unease I felt one little bit.

Was there something to Aladdin's claims?

A noise from somewhere outside of my bedroom drew my attention. It was the sound of Anna bothering something. Usually the noise she was making came to the accompaniment of someone else swearing as she tore a chunk out of their ankle. No such shouts arose though.

'Anna,' I called, hoping she would come. 'Anna, come on girl.' She didn't appear and the sound of her growling continued. Huffing, I got up but as I did so, she came trotting through the door.

With a large snake in her mouth.

To say I was stunned would really fail to capture the emotion I felt when I realised what she was carrying, but that too, paled in comparison when she dropped it and I saw that it was not only still alive, but also rather annoyed.

I don't know much about snakes, but I know a cobra when I see one. It raised its head off the floor in a show of defiance, so Anna dived at it, knocking it down with her tiny paws and instinctively gripping it just behind its head so it couldn't bite her.

Then she carried it over to me, proudly prancing with her prize and keen to show it off. I said, 'Arrrrgh!' which wasn't my most articulate sentence ever. However, it managed to capture all of the emotions I felt quite neatly. 'Mummy doesn't want the snake, sweetie,' I insisted as I jumped off the dressing table chair and backed away. Anna kept coming though, desperate to show her human what she had found.

She dropped it again, the large snake sensing it was beaten this time and making a bid for freedom by darting under my bed. There was no escape from Anna though as she growled and ran after it, ducking when the snake tried to strike her, then coming in underneath it to grab its neck once more.

This time, she gave it a good shake, much like a dog does with a chew toy when excited. The snake reacted badly to being vigorously shaken though; it had more moving parts than a stuffed bear, so this time, when she spat it out, it just rolled onto the marble tile and looked dead.

Because it was.

Ever since I kicked Aladdin out, I had been resisting the urge to call Jermaine. I knew he would come running and the chances were he was struggling with the concept of having a valet to do things for him. Telling myself I couldn't because I would be placing my needs before his had stopped me. Now though, I needed someone to get rid of a snake and no matter what I acknowledged about my life and my spirit changing over the last few weeks, I wasn't picking up the dead cobra.

With my phone in my shaking hand, I dialled the number for his cell. He picked it up as if he had been waiting for it, 'Madam, how can I help you? Do you require my assistance?'

His response dialled back my panic about twelve notches, just hearing his voice made all the difference. 'Jermaine, angel, you need to stop calling me madam. We are very much equals here even if you argue with me about the concept on the Aurelia. I could do with your assistance though, despite what I just said. I have a dead snake on the floor. Is that something you could help me with?'

'I shall be with you momentarily, ma... Mrs Fisher.'

'Try again.'

He sighed deeply before saying, 'I shall be with you momentarily, Patricia.'

'Thank you, Jermaine. I look forward to seeing you.' I clicked the phone off to end the call and looked down to where my Dachshund was still worrying the dead snake. 'Anna, where do you find that?' I asked. I got no answer, of course, just an inquisitive look for a second before she went back to nudging the dead snake with her nose.

A knock at the door broke the spell and jolted me from staring at Anna and the snake. Stifling the need to call out that I was coming, I made my way to the door as swiftly as I could while laughing internally at how slowly Jermaine would have moved were it him answering the door; his determined resistance to hurrying, something that always entertained me.

31

However, when I opened the door to find him in his butler's tails, I could do nothing but sigh. 'You brought the outfit with you?'

He met me with an even gaze. 'I suspected, madam, that it would be needed.' And now I was stuck. A few seconds ago I had pushed him into addressing me by my first name, now he was back in his butler's guise and I already knew there was no way he would address me as anything but madam.

I stopped fighting it. 'The snake's in my bedroom.' Jermaine stepped over the threshold and into my stateroom, one of the few people that could do so without Anna trying to kill them. Not that Anna hadn't tried at the start; she had several goes at ripping Jermaine's ankles to shreds, but he was fast, and he was always so calm. Anna gave up trying to bite him when she got bored with being scooped into the air and cooed at.

Jermaine needed no further encouragement from me. He nodded once and strode into my suite to deal with the offensive serpent's corpse. I heard a toilet flush and that seemed to be that. I hadn't moved far from the door, but I was close enough to hear Jermaine move through my suite and the sound of gas escaping as he opened a bottle. The gas sound was followed by the sound of ice hitting the bottom of a glass and then he reappeared with what was very obviously a gin and tonic in his hand.

Relief washed through me in a surprising way; I hadn't even tasted it yet, but I shot him a raised eyebrow anyway. 'Where's yours?' He opened his mouth to respond, undoubtedly planning to say something butlery, but I shot him down. 'I have no wish to drink alone. Will you join me?' I said it softly; we were friends, even though he liked to pretend our relationship was master and servant.

From behind his back, he produced a second glass and held it up to mine with a smile. Then his lips wobbled, and he glanced down and back up, caught in indecision about what he wanted to say. I gave him a second of silence, then stepped into his personal space to place a hand on his arm. He locked eyes with me then and found his voice, 'Thank you for being my friend, Patricia.'

My breath caught in my chest, an involuntary reaction but the honest one, nevertheless. Somehow, Jermaine and I had grown very close. He was my butler and acted as if it was an absolute privilege to bring me things, yet I knew he felt the same way about me as I did about him. There was nothing sexual in it, yet it was perhaps the closest relationship I had ever experienced with a man.

I could think of nothing to say, so I raised my glass in a salute and took a sip. It was sublime. Then it hit me. 'Where did you find gin in a dry country?'

'I am not without resources.' A large hip flask appeared in his right hand and disappeared again just as quickly. 'Everyone seemed surprised that this was a dry country; I knew already and never thought to question my need to smuggle something in.'

I sipped my gin, sensing that there might not be many of them to come since our supply was limited. Its cold, deep flavours collided with my taste buds like two cars in a head on crash though I resisted the desire to express my pleasure. Instead, I asked, 'So, what do we do now?'

'We get ready to attend the banquet, madam.'

Jermaine was talking to me, but his eyes were following Anna. 'Everything alright?' I asked, wondering what he was looking at.

'Um… Anna is in season. Did you notice?'

'What?' My head shot around to stare at my dog. I guess she had been acting kind of strange recently. 'Are you sure?'

He gave me an amused look. 'Quite sure, madam. I had dogs growing up. The signs are all there.'

It had not occurred to me to question whether she had been spayed or not. She was an adult dog; I knew that much but there was no vet on the Aurelia, so I had taken her to Dr Kim for a quick once over when I first brought her onboard. He declared her fit and well and checked her teeth, at which point she tried to bite him. At no point had her reproductive cycle come up. How often do dogs come into season? I had no idea but didn't think it was something I needed to worry about; it wasn't as if there were any other Dachshunds, or dogs of any kind for that matter, who might wish to... visit with her.

Concerned that she might be feeling a little off colour and grumpy, I picked her up for a cuddle. If we were in our suite on the Aurelia, I would feed her chocolates and put on a Ryan Reynolds movie to watch with a hot water bottle on her belly. As that wasn't an option and I really needed to finish getting ready, I settled her into her bed, patted her head and tucked her up with a blanket. 'Mummy will be back soon,' I told her, but then it really was time to do something about my hair.

Banquet

With a gin that could be used to start an engine inside me, I was ready to face my adoring crowd. Except I wasn't. Not really. The whole concept of being worshipped was freaking me out. I could handle a small amount of adoration; a few thank yous was tolerable, but a banquet thrown by a Maharaja with heads of state from various nations all there to witness my majesty – well, that was too much.

Nevertheless, I was dressed like a fairy-tale princess in the wonderful outfit provided for me. It was made of a luxurious silk that was as soft and cool as a cloud against my skin and they made me look like Princess Jasmine from the Disney *Aladdin* movie. Or, at least, a middle-aged, slightly saggy version of her. Jermaine had expertly crafted my hair into a weave held in place with jewelled pins, once again provided for the event. The reflection in my mirror wasn't everything I wanted it to be – I was fifty-three now I reminded myself more than once. Still, it wasn't terrible either and my outfit for the night was good enough to cover my midriff, a concern that instantly arose when I saw it laid out for me on the bed.

Jermaine reappeared, letting himself back into my suite having departed to get himself ready. He looked like an Arabian prince; his ornate black tunic interwoven with gold thread to match his gold trousers. 'Are you ready, madam? An honour guard is waiting outside to escort you to the banquet.' Like it or not, it was time to go.

I nodded with a grimace. 'Can't put it off any longer. Are the others ready?'

'I have yet to check, madam.'

I crossed the room to check on Anna. She was still sleeping in her bed, disinterested in what the humans were doing. I gave her a pat anyway. 'Let's knock for them on our way, shall we?'

The others had the same idea though because they were knocking on my door before I could get to it. Anna responded in her usual manner, barking and tearing across the marble tile to kill whoever had dared to knock. Barbie's voice cooed back at her through the door, not that it did a thing to calm her down. Jermaine got to my door first, scooping the terror sausage before he opened it.

Outside, were Barbie and Hideki, and Deepa and Martin. Both girls had outfits similar to mine, but they were both happily showing off their taut bellies. They were three decades younger than me, but I still took a moment to grumble internally at the ravages of time. The chaps both wore the same outfit as Jermaine, and each looked a million dollars. Beyond my friends was a six-man honour guard wearing ceremonial robes.

'Ready to go?' Deepa asked.

'Any sign of the Hawaiians?' I asked in return, peering along the corridor to see where they were.

'We thought they might be with you,' replied Barbie, her brow wrinkling. 'We got no answer from their doors.'

I took Anna from Jermaine, intending to put her back into her bed, but a dog bark echoed out from another stateroom further down the passageway and she wriggled in my grip, breaking free and bouncing down to the marble floor as she escaped me.

'Anna!' I called after her as she zipped between Hideki's feet and took off. I called her name again, but she had other things on her mind,

36

reaching a door further down the passageway which then barked at her as she whined at it.

'What's got into her?' asked Barbie as I set off to fetch the errant little dog.

'She's in season,' Jermaine explained, which elicited a knowing response from everyone waiting outside my stateroom. How was it everyone knew about this except me?

Anna was pawing at the door and alternating that with sniffing underneath it. I could hear the sound of dogs sniffing from the other side but before I could get to Anna the door opened and she barged through the gap. She didn't get very far though, a man on the other side expertly scooped her into the air even as she tried to get to the dogs inside.

'Hello,' he said, holding her in front of his face with both hands. Around his feet and jumping up at his legs, were half a dozen Corgis. His gaze switched from Anna to me as I arrived. He said, 'Hello,' again. 'Is this little lady yours?'

'Yes, sorry,' I replied, my cheeks colouring slightly. 'I think it best if I take her away.' And maybe fit her with a chastity belt, I thought as he handed her over. He was dressed in what I took to be butler's livery, but his delicate English accent and the presence of the Corgis made me wonder who he worked for. I didn't ask though, instead I gratefully accepted the wriggling Anna, who was still trying to get to the male dogs circling her below. Then I thanked the man and left him to wrangle the overexcited Corgis back inside.

'Whose room is that?' asked Barbie, her eyes wide in wonder.

I didn't want to think too much about who might have been inside the stateroom. 'He didn't say,' I told her, which was an honest answer though I suspected I could guess.

Barbie and everyone else waited for me as I placed Anna back in her bed. The little dog wore a grumpy expression, clearly disgruntled that I had stopped her fun though I was sure she would forgive me. Finally back in the passageway where the captain of the honour guard was beginning to look impatient, it was time to set off. Just as we started walking, another door opened a little further down the passageway, a couple emerging arm in arm.

'Isn't that the French Prime Minister?' asked Martin, his eyes bugging out of his head a little. Panic swirled around my stomach again; who was I to be getting honoured tonight in front of all these important people?

Wanting as many people by my side as possible, I hammered on Rick's door as we passed it. 'I expect they just fell asleep.' No answer came though and no sound either. Where was his valet? I might have dismissed mine, but surely Rick's would be in attendance.

'Could they have already gone down without us?' asked Deepa. Martin was at Akamu's door and getting as much response from it as I was from Rick's. I shrugged. There was no way of answering the question until we found them.

With no other options, we proceeded without them, following the honour guard along the wide passageway. It was a good thing they came for us though; we would never have found our way without them. The banquet was inside the palace, in a huge room filled with exotic plants and exotic people. Musicians were playing what I guessed to be traditional Zangrabarian instruments, but the tune, which I recognised to be *Jive Talking* by the Beegees, stopped as my honour guard entered the

38

vast hall. In its place, a fanfare erupted with a blast of deafening noise. Buglers, the same ones I had seen at the airstrip, were trumpeting my arrival. It felt quite medieval, but it killed all conversation in the room as all eyes swung my way and spontaneous applause sprang up around the room. Was I supposed to bow?

I could feel my cheeks beginning to glow from all the unwanted attention, but there was no escape now. The clomp, clomp, clomp of the vizier's staff announced his arrival before he emerged from the crowd. 'Good evening, Your Eminence,' he said with a broad smile on his face. Then he turned around to face the room. 'Your Majesty, Maharaja Zebradim, Lords and Marshalls of our armed forces, assembled distinguished guests from around the globe, please raise a toast to tonight's most honoured guest, a person without whom we would not be able to hold the coronation tomorrow. I give you Zangrabar's saviour, Her Eminence, Mrs Patricia Fisher.'

Many of the people staring at me gave polite applause, but most of those I would pick out as being Zangrabarian nationals, whooped and cheered like we were at a football game and I just scored the winning goal. Then the crowd parted and once again the Maharaja floated toward me on his bed of cushions.

'Mrs Fisher, please join me at the head of the table.' Without uttering a command, the men bearing his bed stopped walking and lowered it to the floor so he could get off. In a fluid motion, he stood up and reached out with his right hand to guide me. The applause continued as I followed him to the grand table.

It wasn't really a table though; it was a low platform with cushions arranged around it for everyone to sit on. I had seen people eating like this on television or in National Geographic magazine, I hadn't ever experienced it for myself though. Sitting down for the meal, I was

39

concerned about a number of things: Would my host be polite and engaging or a horny teenage brat? Would I like the food? Would I be expected to make a speech, or would I come face to face with the Queen of Spain and be unable to come up with anything sensible to say?

All those concerns vanished though when I realised I still hadn't seen Rick and Akamu. Where were they? I leaned forward to stare down the length of the table. It was arranged in a horseshoe shape with two legs and a top table with the Maharaja in the centre and me to his right.

'Is everything alright, my dear?' asked a man to my right as he too took his seat. When I looked up at him, he said, 'Lord Edgar Postlewaite at your service, ma'am. I'm the British Ambassador in these here parts.' Lord Postlewaite was nearing sixty, his high breeding resulting in a weak chin, watery eyes and a bald scalp. He had a nice smile though.

I glanced at him but only briefly. I was still scouring the assembled persons for any sign of my two missing friends. 'Some of my friends are missing,' I muttered, craning my neck to see. 'I haven't seen them since we arrived a few hours ago.'

The ambassador swivelled his head and lifted an arm, which summoned a young man in a suit to his side without the need for verbal communication. He spoke to him though I didn't hear what he said, and the man hurried away. 'Jared will investigate, my dear. Now,' he turned to give me his full attention, 'tell me all about the giant sapphire and how it was that you came to have it in your possession.'

The question was overheard by more than a dozen people sitting in close proximity, so, yet again, focus swung to me, expectation palpable. I didn't feel like I had any choice but to tell the story now, but the young Maharaja made it impossible for me to do anything else. 'Yes, Mrs Fisher.

40

Please entertain me and my guests. I am sure everyone is truly curious to hear your tale.'

I swallowed and took a sip of water to wet my dry mouth, cursed that there was no gin and smiled at my audience as I took them back to the morning I found Jack Langley dead in his cabin. Food was served while I talked, course after course of exotic breads, pastries, stuffed meats, sweet fruit teas and more. I didn't get to eat any of it because I was talking, but I managed to fill a plate that I could tuck into when I got to the end of the story.

Further down the table, people were still talking but as I continued, more and more of them fell silent and moved toward me, dragging their cushions with them so they could hear what I was saying. I got to the end and jumped forward to the part where the telegram arrived because it provided a neat conclusion. '...and that is how I come to be here today. I stress the point that recovering the sapphire was a team effort though. Miss Barbara Berkeley, Mr Jermaine Clarke and Mr Martin Baker all played key roles in solving the mystery. I could not have done it without them.'

As I fell silent and reached for my glass of water again, rapturous applause erupted, embarrassing me again. Hoping that everyone would now see I was eating and thus not ask me questions; I selected a flatbread coated in a spicy couscous and popped it in my mouth.

The ambassador leaned in to speak to me as the applause subsided, 'That was quite incredible, my dear. And you told the story with such passion.' Then he placed his left hand on my upper thigh and I almost spat out my food.

He saw my reaction and removed his hand. 'Too soon. My apologies, Mrs Fisher, I'm afraid I am finding it hard to control myself. You are quite the filly, you see, and it has been a long time since I last met an eligible English woman.'

A filly? I pierced him with a hard stare. 'Well you can consider me ineligible, thank you very much. I shall thank you for keeping your hands to yourself from now on.'

My rebuke only seemed to encourage him though. 'Yowzer!' he growled, making a noise like a tiger. 'So feisty. I shall do my best to keep up.'

My mouth dropped open as I prepared to berate him for not listening, then chose a different option and turned to speak to the Maharaja instead, giving the ambassador my back. 'Your Majesty, I have a question for you if you would be so kind.'

His attention had been on the crowd in the room, surveying his subjects and honoured guests but he looked at me as I drew his focus. 'Of course, Mrs Fisher. I shall do my best to answer.'

Reminding myself that I was speaking to the ruler of an entire nation and not a teenage boy, I formed the question in my head. Then I saw him glance at my boobs and just asked it anyway. 'In the telegram I received, it suggested you had a mystery you wished me to look into while I am here. I asked the vizier about it, but he didn't know.'

The young king looked worried for a moment, his eyes flaring as if startled or caught in a lie and I felt a twinge of panic myself as I thought I might have somehow insulted him. On his other side sat his uncle, Prince Zebrahim. He leaned in to whisper something in his nephew's ear then straightened again to continue his previous conversation. The concerned look passed from the Maharaja's face almost instantly, gone as if it were never there. 'I'm sorry, Mrs Fisher. That need has been resolved,' he replied with a contented smile. 'Thank you for your kind offer. My only

42

desire for your stay here is that you feel the gratitude of Zangrabar and leave us knowing that you will always be welcome back.' I bowed my head at his kind words. 'I have a question for you though.'

I gave him my full attention. 'I hope I can answer.'

He glanced down the table, and then pointed. 'Your blonde friend with the impressive rack. Is she available? I would very much like her to join my harem.' Not for the first time in his company, I felt my jaw drop open. 'Her dark-skinned friend is impressive too. Do they do a double act, do you know?'

'Um,' I spluttered. Had he been anyone else I would have emptied a glass of ice-cold water over his head or maybe just slapped his face. He had remained polite and regal while people were listening but had returned to his horny teenage boy persona now that attention was off him.

'You're right, Mrs Fisher,' he said, taking my lack of answer as an answer in itself, 'I should ask them myself. That way I can impress them with my bank account, show them some diamonds and...' He got a faraway look in his eyes that made me wonder what might be happening three feet south of his mouth. Thankfully, he chose that moment to clap his hands together twice. The action drew the attention of a hundred servants, the master of ceremony and most of the guests. 'It is time for merriment!' he shouted loudly and sprang to his feet as musicians began playing once more.

Large curtains to my right, which I believed were hiding nothing more than a wall, swept aside to reveal another vast room. This one was filled with dancing girls, men juggling flaming torches and all manner of other exotica to entice and delight. The Maharaja extended his hand to me, inviting me to go with him as the master of ceremony called everyone else to join us for the night's festivities.

I let the young Maharaja lead me through to the other room, but I spared a glance back at the banquet table; it was still covered in food and all around were confused faces, wondering what had just happened: dinner wasn't finished. I wasn't even sure all the food had been served yet but the ruler of the country had decreed that the formal part of the evening was over, so it was.

The back of my skull gave an itch: there was something screwy going on.

Whether it was normal custom to interrupt a meal, the whim of a young and poorly mannered man with too much power, or something else entirely, the guests at the banquet, heads of nations, famous people and VIPs, played along without complaint.

As they relaxed, mingled and enjoyed the music and entertainment, I waited for the Maharaja to be distracted by someone else and then drifted away to find Barbie and Jermaine. Rick and Akamu were still unaccounted for and I was beginning to get an uncomfortable lump in my stomach.

Spotting my friends through the press of people, I started across the room toward them. I didn't get very far though before Lord Postlewaite blocked my path. 'Lady Fisher.'

'That's Mrs Fisher,' I replied coolly.

'Only until our wedding, dear lady. Then it shall be Lady Patricia Postlewaite. It has such a perfect ring to it. We shall be very happy, you and I. Certainly I shall, given how saucy you are. Shall we escape these walls and take a walk outside? I know where some dark corners can be found.'

I rolled my eyes and thought about dumping a bucket of ice-water on his head. 'I'm looking for my friends still. Remember them? The two chaps I told you hadn't been seen since we arrived. Didn't your man Jared take off to find them?'

'Oh, yes. I shouldn't worry my dear. There's not much trouble they can get themselves into. Not unless they went looking for alcohol.' He saw the flicker of doubt in my eyes. 'Ah. Well, if they are so inclined, there are plenty of places one can find it. Most usually one also finds the company of ladies of negotiable pleasure. If they are not here, I am sure that will be where they are.'

I thought about that for about half a second. They were men and I knew that even when you thought you knew a person, you never really do, but I couldn't see the two of them taking off to find a brothel.

'Hi, Patty,' said Barbie, appearing by my side with Hideki's hand gripped in hers. Jermaine, Martin, and Deepa were right behind her. 'Hello,' she said to Lord Postlewaite, 'I'm Barbie.'

'I dare say you are, my dear,' he replied and laughed at a joke that no one else understood.

I rolled my eyes again. Then introduced him. 'This is the British Ambassador to Zangrabar, Lord Postlewaite. Have any of you seen Rick or Akamu?'

Jermaine spoke up. 'No, madam. I believe I should begin a search for them and request one of the staff let us into their rooms so we can check there.'

I agreed entirely. I glanced about, wondered how soon I would be missed if I snuck out and decided I was too concerned about my friends to care if I was missed for a while. I could always return later and claim to have felt ill and in need of a lie down. 'Come on,' I said as I headed for the exit. 'Let's both go.'

'Shouldn't we all go?' asked Martin.

I shook my head. 'I think it will draw attention if we all leave together and might appear rude. Perhaps just Jermaine and I should go. If we find them, we will come straight back.' They saw the wisdom of my suggestion and agreed to stay, which left Jermaine and I with the task of getting into

Rick and Akamu's rooms. I hoped to find each of them asleep on their beds, but I doubted I would.

As luck would have it, I ran into the man in the sharp suit from the airstrip as we left the banquet. I tried to remember his name, but it wouldn't come to me. He was working, not taking part in the festivities and crossed in front of me going from one room to another in the passageway outside.

'Hello,' I called to get his attention, his head and eyes swinging in my direction even as his feet carried him onward.

'Your Eminence,' he replied as he stopped walking. He looked startled to see me. 'Leaving the banquet so soon?'

As I opened my mouth to speak, my brain did me a favour and supplied his name, so I didn't have to look ignorant. 'Osama, two of my friends are missing. The two older gentlemen from my party. No one has seen them since we arrived. Can you arrange to have their rooms opened for me? They are not answering their doors, their valets appear to have gone AWOL and I am becoming concerned.'

He understood the urgency of my request with no further explanation required. 'Please give me just a moment, Your Eminence.' Then he used his phone to speak to someone in a rapid-fire exchange of words. As he hung up, he started moving. 'Please come with me. Someone will meet us at their rooms.'

Jermaine and I hurried after him. The palace at night was quite beautiful and the grounds outside enticing now that the temperature had dropped. We found out how nice it was when the man led us through a door and into the gardens. The lush tropical paradise was backlit by the stars above and accompanied by the sound of water falling from the many fountains.

47

'This is the shortest route back to your staterooms,' he explained as we crossed the grass and went back inside through a different door. He was walking fast, not that it was difficult to keep up, but it was as if he were more concerned than I about the odd absence of my two retired friends.

As we passed a mosaic I recognised and drew close to our accommodations, Jermaine gently tapped my arm. 'Madam, we are being followed.' A spark of fear shot through me, but I resisted the urge to turn and look. 'I cannot see who it is,' Jermaine whispered, 'but I believe it is one person. They are sticking to the shadows, but not very well, which just makes them easier to spot.'

I nodded my understanding but said nothing; we had arrived at Akamu's door where a servant in palace livery was waiting for us. The doors were fitted with biometric state-of-the-art hand-scanning locks which we now needed to override. He achieved that simply enough by inserting an electronic key and placing his palm on the panel. The door clicked open.

Osama Al-Kaisi wasted no time, pushing the door wide open as he marched into Akamu's room. 'Mr Kameāloha, are you here, sir? Fariq, please attend.'

Coming through the door behind him I added my own voice, 'Akamu.' Neither my friend nor his valet answered though. The suite of rooms was empty.

'We should check Mr Hutton's suite as well,' Osama said as he turned back toward the front entrance.

I was in Akamu's bedroom though, checking on a few things. 'One moment,' I called to him as I poked about. Akamu's clothes from the day were discarded in a corner, which meant he had changed and most likely taken the time to shower or bathe, and his outfit for the banquet was nowhere to be found, so he had changed into it. At least, that felt like a safe assumption. If he and Rick had intended to go elsewhere as the ambassador suggested, they would have worn normal clothing, not gold pants.

Osama joined me in the bedroom. 'What are you looking for, Your Eminence?'

In reply I pointed out the evidence of Akamu's movements. It didn't really mean anything yet, but he was missing, and I was going to struggle to believe he simply went off on an adventure instead of attending the banquet he came here for. What did that mean though? I set off for Rick's suite, my stride purposeful and I left Osama behind in my haste so he had to rush to catch up.

He had a question as we went out the door, 'What is going on, Your Eminence? Where are your friends?'

Reaching the passageway outside, I saw that Jermaine had already gone into Rick's stateroom. I didn't have an answer for Osama's question yet, but a creeping sensation of doubt and worry began invading my thoughts. I could hear conversation from within; Jermaine's deep rumbling voice echoing from somewhere mixed with at least two other voices.

We found them in the servant's area, a room filled with cleaning products and other items they might need. Jermaine looked up as I approached. 'Madam, the valets claim Mr Hutton and Mr Kameāloha went out.' It was clear from his tone that he didn't believe them.

With their eyes cast down, both men looked apologetic, as if the actions of Rick and Akamu were somehow their fault. Both men wore simple robes in a cream shade, much the same as Aladdin's with a turban to match his as well. They were very similar in height, weight and

49

appearance and could have been brothers for all I knew. The one closest to Jermaine spoke. 'Mr Hutton insisted that he needed a drink. I assured him there was no alcohol to be found but he refused to believe me.'

His colleague chipped in his part of the story, 'Mr Kameāloha said there would be places to drink at the docks, that sailors always had alcohol and they could find what they needed there. He kept saying it was Jack and coke time.' It sounded exactly like something the boys would say, but I didn't believe what I was being told.

Osama did though, shaking his head in disappointment. 'Why did you not report this?' he demanded of the two valets, his voice hard. 'The security forces should have been informed the moment they left the palace.' With their eyes still staring firmly at the marble tiles, both men looked more miserable than before, but they had no answer. He turned to me now, concern on his face. 'I will do what I can, Mrs Fisher, but if your friends are caught in possession of alcohol or return to the streets of Zangrabar in a state of inebriation, they will be arrested and incarcerated.'

'What is the punishment for inebriation here?' I asked, worried that I might not like the answer.

He grimaced before he answered. 'Public flogging.'

I grimaced too. I still didn't believe that my friends were so desperate for a drink they elected to abscond in search of it. Evidence wasn't in my favour though. I made eye contact with Jermaine, the exchange of looks sufficient to tell me he didn't believe it either. I couldn't say that though, not until I knew more about what was going on.

Instead I said, 'We should head back to the banquet.'

Jermaine nodded his head. 'Very good, madam.'

Osama looked at his watch, made a small noise of displeasure and started toward the door of the suite. 'I shall have to report this, I'm afraid. I hope for your friends' sake that they failed in their quest to find alcohol.'

I couldn't think of anything to say; thoughts were swirling about my head, all of which argued against the idea that the guys absconded. We were back outside in the passageway now though and about to return to the party. I stopped, drawing Jermaine's attention as I did. 'I'm going to check on Anna since we are up here.' When Osama raised an eyebrow at me, I explained, 'That's my little dog. She caught a cobra earlier. I don't like to think that there might be another one.'

Now Osama eyed me curiously, causing my feet to stop just as I started toward my suite. 'A cobra?'

'Yes. Big thing, hood behind its head.'

'Surely you must be mistaken, Your Eminence.'

'Why is that?'

'There are no cobras in Zangrabar. Asps, boas, all manner of other snakes, but never a cobra.'

Sensing what that meant, I said, 'My mistake. Come along, Jermaine,' and went to my suite.

As we neared the door and were out of Osama's earshot, Jermaine whispered, 'That means someone put the snake in your suite, madam.'

'Yup.' I didn't like it, but it was the only conclusion I could draw. My friends were missing, and someone had put a deadly snake in my room. I wanted to panic and run away now, get a taxi, go to the airport and leave the country before something truly bad happened but with Rick and Akamu missing I couldn't go anywhere. Instead, I was going to have to work out what the heck was happening, get my friends back and get everyone out of here in one piece if I could. 'You spotted someone following us,' I reminded my butler.

'Yes, madam,' he replied calmly. 'Whoever it is, they are fifty yards behind us and followed us all the way from the banquet.'

I placed my hand on the biometric scanner to open my door. As it clicked open, I hatched a quick plan and shared it with Jermaine. Anna bounded across the marble floor as I pushed the door open, her claws skittering to announce her approach. She was still alive and there was no evidence of further snake attack, so I guess she had just slept while I was out. She didn't stop when she got to me though, she was heading for the open door and planned to escape.

From down the passageway came a howl which was joined by others as the Corgis got a whiff of my ripe Dachshund. Jermaine, his reflexes like lightning, snagged her before she could get away and once again, we foiled her plans.

I carried her back inside, leaving the door open behind me, then moved further into the suite with Anna tucked under my arm. The mystery shadow had tailed me this far but would he or she be bold enough to follow me into my stateroom? Whatever their plan, I doubted they had followed me to hand out coupons and I wanted to know what threat they intended.

My mystery shadow took their time, nervousness or trepidation perhaps slowing their pace as they approached to such an extent that I wanted to shout for them to hurry up. Eventually, the shadow plucked up the courage to sneak into my room though, stealing a glance or two around the doorframe before finally stepping over the threshold. The lights in the lobby were off deliberately, creating shadows and dark corners. Partly this was to encourage the person in, but it was also to hide Jermaine.

The tall Jamaican had settled himself into a dark spot behind the door where he would be obscured from view despite his large size. I made sure I was in sight but deeper into the suite and conducting a conversation with an imaginary person, so the person following me would assume Jermaine and I were both in the same room.

I had one eye on the door though and saw the shadow pass through the rectangle of light there. I didn't see Jermaine move though I did hear a cry of shock and a noise that sounded rather like, 'Urk!' as Jermaine imposed his martial arts skills to subdue the intruder.

I rushed to the lobby and threw the light switch. Jermaine had his knee on the neck of a man in court dress and the man's arm hooked up into the air at an improbable angle. Anna was struggling to free herself from my grip; there was a new person she needed to terrorise.

From his position on the floor, the man said through his smooshed mouth, 'I say, Mrs Fisher, could you see your way to having your man release me? This is awfully uncomfortable.'

I crossed my arms and stared down at the British ambassador. 'Ambassador, why were you following me?' I suspected I already knew the answer.

He tried a smile, but with half his face pressed flat against the floor it just made him look creepy. It made me relent. With a despondent smile, I said, 'It's okay, Jermaine. Let him up.'

'If you are sure, madam,' he replied as he released the ambassador's arm and stepped back. Then, like the true gentleman he is, Jermaine helped his fallen opponent back to his feet. 'Are you alright, sir,' he asked, brushing dust from the ambassador's suit.

Flippantly the ambassador answered, 'Yes, quite well, thank you. If you could just help me to get my shoulder back into its socket...'

I grabbed his collar, dismissing his daft request because his shoulder was fine. 'Why were you following me? And what have you done with my friends?'

Lord Edgar flapped his lips a few times as he fought for an answer. 'I'm... I'm sorry, Mrs Fisher, I thought I made my intention to woo you obvious earlier. I hoped I might make a more succinct plea in private.'

I couldn't prevent the incredulous look that arrived on my face. 'You followed me back to my room in the hope that you might bed me?'

He struggled for an answer again, then his brow knitted as a question formed. 'Your friends are still missing? The same ones from earlier?'

'Yes,' I snapped, my annoyance and frustration manifesting as impatience. 'Their valets claim they went to the docks to look for alcohol.'

'But you don't believe them?'

'Would you go to the docks in ceremonial dress? Ask sailors for a drink wearing loose-fitting gold pants?'

Lord Edgar inclined his head, acknowledging my point. 'I guess I wouldn't. They could have changed their clothes though. How sure are you that they went to the docks in their ceremonial clothes?'

Now it was my turn to concede a point; I had no evidence either way. 'I can't be certain.'

'Then we must pray they failed to find what they sought. There is no leniency here, that is something I know for certain. If caught they will not be offered a trial, punishment will take place within a few days.'

I was getting angry. Not at Rick and Akamu; I still didn't believe they were guilty. It was the situation that was driving me nuts. Lord Edgar hadn't taken offense at being thrown on the marble tile thankfully. In fact, he looked to be invigorated by the experience.

'Shall we return to the banquet, madam?' asked Jermaine standing patiently by the door.

I nodded my head. 'I'll just put Anna back to bed.'

A minute later, with that task complete, three of us left my suite on route back to the Maharaja and his merriment.

We got about three yards.

Problems

I recognised that the man running toward us and looking threatening was Jared, the ambassador's man, about a half second after I saw Jermaine duck into a defensive crouch. My butler was ready to defend me against whatever attack might be about to occur, but I grabbed his arm to stay him.

'Sir,' Jared called loudly, paying little attention to Jermaine as he focused on the ambassador. He was out of breath and looked flustered. I kept quiet so I would hear what he had to say. 'I found them, sir,' Jared reported.

Lord Edgar beamed at him. 'Jolly well done, dear fellow. Where are they?'

'In jail, sir.'

I said a rude word, my cheeks colouring when everyone looked at me. 'You're going to tell me they are drunk, aren't you?' I demanded.

The ambassador's man glanced at me and then at the ambassador and then back at me. 'Yes, ma'am. Drunk as lords in fact. No offense, sir,' he added quickly with an embarrassed glance at Lord Edgar.

I squinted at him. 'Did you see them?'

'Yes, ma'am. I wasn't able to speak with them though.'

'Because they are American?'

'No, ma'am. Because they were unconscious from the alcohol.'

'Oh, dear,' said Lord Edgar.

I just shook my head though. 'This is a set up,' I declared adamantly. 'There is no way either one of them would slip out of the palace and dodge the banquet in search of alcohol and absolutely no way they would drink themselves into oblivion.'

'Have you known these men for a long time?' the ambassador asked.

I gritted my teeth because it was the perfect question to ask if a person wanted to trash my argument. I had known Rick and Akamu for no more than a few weeks, but I was certain I knew them; that I knew their personalities. I didn't bother to answer Lord Edgar; I could gain nothing from doing so. Instead, I started walking.

Jermaine fell into step next to me. 'Madam, I wish to advise caution.' I gave him my side eye; a narrow squint designed to suggest he exercise caution himself. 'If we are to rescue Mr Hutton and Mr Kameāloha, it may be necessary to observe who the players are first.' Okay, he was making sense, so I forced my rising ire to calm while he continued to speak. 'We are without friends or back up here. The ambassador seems genuine, but we have no reason to trust him yet and I fear there may be events in play that we are not aware of yet.'

I reached out to touch his arm. 'Thank you, Jermaine. You are, of course, quite correct. We should inform the others, act surprised and concerned but observe rather than attempting to do anything more productive at this time.' Jermaine hit our problem on the nose when he talked about identifying the players; we had no idea what was going on, only that Rick and Akamu were incarcerated and someone had placed a snake in my room. When you add that to the fact that our plane was almost shot out of the sky on the way here, it started to look like a conspiracy was in progress.

All this swirled through my head as we made our way back to the banquet. I arrived intending to find Barbie and the others, however, as I came through the curtain and back into the huge room with the dancers, musicians, fire eaters, and more, the first thing I saw was the Maharaja. In the middle of the dancefloor, egged on by dozens of eligible-looking young women, the young king was twerking and soaking up the attention while the VIPs and statesmen from around the world looked on with barely contained expressions of surprise.

Aladdin's warning echoed in my head once more: Maybe the problem I faced was bigger than I thought.

Nocturnal Activities

Now anxious about my friends and paranoid about the snake Anna found in my suite, I accepted a drink when it was offered but didn't drink it, electing to go thirsty rather than risk imbibing poison (I said I was getting paranoid, right?). Jermaine and I had a quiet word with Barbie, Hideki, Martin and Deepa, keeping smiles on our faces and telling the others to react with a laugh just in case anyone was watching.

Seriously paranoid. Unless someone really was out to get us, in which case we were being prudently cautious and wise. All I said to them was that Rick and Akamu had been found and were probably in trouble because they had gone out looking for alcohol. I didn't want to tell them about the punishment that might await them once they were sober; it would ruin the evening and I didn't warn them not to eat or drink anything. If someone wanted us dead by poison, they could have easily done it already.

'You think the boys will be alright?' asked Barbie.

I had no wish to trouble her or anyone else until I knew more, so I lied, 'Yes. I expect they will sleep it off and be handed back to us when we head to the plane.'

She considered what I said but didn't give it much thought; she was distracted by Hideki whose arm was around her waist. 'Silly guys. They missed all this fun.' She was talking about the entertainment laid on for the banquet's guests and she was right, they had missed it. So had I though and I had little interest in it now because I was too sick with worry.

Servants were circling the hall with trays of drinks, all sweet teas and fruit concoctions and super-sweet coffee. I kept the one I had in my hand to maintain the image that I was enjoying myself. I didn't want to ruin

Barbie's night or anyone else's by passing my worries onto them. For all I knew, Rick and Akamu were genuinely drunk and the snake had escaped from an Indian delegation staying in a nearby suite.

Across the room, the Maharaja had retired to lie on a raised platform where he could overlook the festivities below. Behind him and standing, his uncle looked on as well. Neither one appeared to be having any fun and the young king looked thoroughly bored now. As I watched him, the light from a phone illuminated his face to show that he was paying no attention to the party or his guests and I wondered if he was checking in on Facebook or playing a game. Either would be typical teenage behaviour in my opinion and the sort of thing he must have been exposed to during his time in America.

I wanted to do something about Rick and Akamu but I couldn't come up with anything proactive at this time. Did I have enough credit to appeal directly to the Maharaja? The idea made my stomach turn but I swallowed my rising butterflies and started in his direction. Surrounding him were half a dozen burly guards, each dressed in traditional garb with wide, black flowing pants and sleeveless white tunics plus a black turban on their heads. They also all had handguns holstered to their right hips and the curly wire of a radio visible as it wrapped around their left ears. Two of them moved to block my path as they saw my intention to approach the Maharaja.

A meaty arm came up with a flat palm toward me; its intention to keep me back or turn me around quite clear. Behind him, the Maharaja clapped his hands twice, the sound making the guard with the raised arm instantly turn his head.

'Mrs Fisher, please join me,' the young king called above the noise of the room. Then he moved to make space for me on the wide bed of cushions.

The guard stepped aside with a nod of his head in my direction and I lifted the hem of my dress to mount the steps more easily and not trip on it. The Maharaja's raised platform was about five feet above the floor, which placed his head above everyone else once he sat up. I checked my footing once more, desperate to not fall on my arse as I approached the king, then met his smile with my own. 'Thank you for seeing me, Your Majesty.'

'Not at all, Mrs Fisher. I am pleased that you would join me. Was there something specific you wanted to discuss with me?' He was talking more normally now though his accent still sounded very similar to Barbie's to my untrained ear and out of place for the ruler of an Arabian nation.

I didn't say that, of course, I settled onto the cushions and prepared a carefully worded question in my head. 'Your Majesty, I wondered if I might ask you again about the mystery your telegram mentioned. It was thoughtless of me to ask you about it during dinner when so many other people were able to listen. If I embarrassed you in any way, I am truly sorry.'

The young man smiled kindly at me. 'Babe.' There was the teenager again. 'You worry too much. I'm afraid there is no mystery for you to solve here.'

Before I could say anything else, I got a sense that someone had moved into my personal space. Then a voice came from behind me, 'Why is it that you ask again, Mrs Fisher?'

I turned to find the Maharaja's uncle looming over me. One eyebrow raised in curiosity, he looked more impatient than anything and I sensed my status as a national treasure didn't sit too well with him. I needed to provide an answer though as both the Prince and the Maharaja were waiting for me to speak. However, this was the bit that worried me when I decided to approach him. 'I have no wish to cause offense, Your Majesty,' I started, addressing the king and not his uncle. 'Earlier this evening, there was a snake in my room.'

'We have many snakes in Zangrabar, Mrs Fisher,' replied the Maharaja's uncle, managing to keep his tone neutral though I was sure he wanted to scoff. 'Even with our best intentions, one will slip inside the place every now and then.'

'This was not an indigenous snake. It was a cobra.'

'Impossible.' This time he did scoff.

The Maharaja berated him though, 'Uncle, please. Remember your manners. Mrs Fisher is our most honoured guest.' Then he turned his gaze back to me. 'Please continue. I'm sure you had more you wished to share with me than the presence of a surprising reptile.'

I nodded my thanks, glanced at the uncle to see if he would interrupt again, and started talking, yet again picking my words carefully. 'Two of my friends went missing earlier this evening.'

Once again, the uncle spoke over me, 'Yes, we know of it. They broke one of this country's most sacred laws. It is only your status that prevented the police from questioning whether you and the rest of your party might be complicit.'

This time the Maharaja did not speak against his older relative; he was tight-lipped when he said, 'If you hoped to appeal against their arrest and the probable punishment they face after trial, then I must advise you that I will not overrule on matters of religion or law. They have broken both by first drinking alcohol on Zangrabarian soil and then by appearing in the streets in a very drunken state. I am deeply saddened that their behaviour has marred your visit, Mrs Fisher, but I would counsel you to distance yourself from them.'

Now I had to argue. 'But I know these men. They are my friends and I cannot believe they would commit any of the crimes they are accused of.'

'What are you suggesting, Mrs Fisher?' asked the Maharaja's uncle. He was leading me into a trap, that much I was sure of; offering me the chance to suggest we were being treated unfairly and thus insult both the Maharaja and the country of Zangrabar.

I bowed my head in supplication toward the Maharaja. 'Your Majesty, I am not suggesting anything. I am concerned though that given the attack on your private jet earlier today, the unexplained snake that is not found in this country, and now my friends break a law when they are both career police officers, something is amiss and I feel that my friends and I may be in danger.' There, I had said it. Now I had to see if he would be insulted and order my decapitation or not.

The uncle opened his mouth to speak, but the Maharaja raised a hand to stop him. 'This is most concerning, Mrs Fisher. Your concern, that is. Your visit to my country should be one of relaxation and enjoyment. The attack on my private jet is being investigated by my security forces as we speak. Initial intelligence suggests it was a private terrorist organisation hoping to cripple my aircraft and force it to land so they could take me hostage and demand a huge reward. They were not to know that I was not on it. I can only apologise that your life was in danger. I believe the snake is just a snake and as for your friends... they were found inebriated after declaring their intention to look for alcohol. I am unsure where you can find anything suspicious in that.'

He paused so that I might counter, but there was nothing I could say, and he knew it. With my head still bowed, I apologised again. 'I have taken up too much of your precious time with my frivolous concerns, Your Majesty. Please forgive me.'

'It should be you who forgives me, Mrs Fisher. You are the honoured guest in my country, and I should have done more to prevent these events from transpiring. I intended your visit to be a celebration.'

He was being more generous than he needed to be and even though I was getting nowhere and still felt certain that something was going on, I had to concede. 'Thank you, Your Majesty. Your country is as beautiful as the people in it. It is my great honour to visit here and to be your guest. On behalf of my entire party, I wish to express my deep gratitude for your generosity and my deep regret for the actions of my friends now awaiting trial.'

'Thank you, Mrs Fisher. Now, if you will excuse me, I must retire. You see it is a Zangrabarian tradition that no one leaves before the Maharaja; if I stay all night, so must everyone else and that would not be fair.' The young man clapped his hands twice and five of the six guards moved to grab handles around the bed we were lying on. The sixth guard leaned in to offer me his hand, then helped me to my feet.

I stepped off the bed of cushions and took a pace back before bowing. The Maharaja was borne into the air and carried away through a set of curtains behind the raised platform.

Once he was lost from sight, I breathed a deep sigh. Nothing had gone according to plan since I got off the Aurelia. More than ever, I wanted to get back to the ship and to Alistair. Somehow though, I needed to rescue Rick and Akamu and to do that I was going to need help. The British ambassador would have no influence over the rights of two American citizens, but I hoped he might be golfing buddies with the US ambassador, or at least have the man's phone number.

Scanning the room failed to reveal him though. Neither he nor his man, Jared, were to be seen. For that matter I couldn't see Barbie or Jermaine or any of the others either. While I was talking with the Maharaja, the rest of my friends had vanished.

As I climbed back up to the Maharaja's raised platform for a better view, my heart began to thump in my chest.

I felt the world spin beneath my feet and for a brief moment my rising panic made me feel faint, but then I spotted Jermaine, the tall Jamaican man surprisingly difficult to spot in the dimly lit room. Having found him, my eyes tracked to the left to see Deepa Bhukari and Martin Baker. I clambered down from the raised platform to go to them.

'Where's Barbie and Hideki?' I asked, failing to keep the concern from my voice.

Jermaine, his head above everyone else in the room, looked about, but shrugged. 'She and Hideki were keeping to themselves, perhaps they are just out of sight. Is there any news of Mr Hutton and Mr Kameāloha?'

'Nothing good. It would seem that everyone knows about them and no one will do anything. I want to appeal to the US ambassador to step in.'

'That won't be possible, I'm afraid,' interjected Lord Edgar, appearing by my side yet again.

I rounded on him. 'Why ever not?'

He raised his eyebrows. 'Because there is no US embassy, dear lady. There hasn't been for more than twenty years after an oil and mineral deal went bad and the US cut them off. It hasn't had much of an impact on the nation's economy so far. Lack of US backing made them spend more on defence which created a lot of jobs and they buy only Russian or Chinese weapons and munitions, so our American cousins really cut their own noses off,' he laughed. Right. No US embassy. That really didn't help. The ambassador wasn't done though. 'I thought I might entice you into a little nightcap? All this non-alcoholic nonsense really makes the evenings drag.'

I eyed him suspiciously. 'You have got to be kidding. My friends are to be publicly punished for drinking and you are offering me alcohol?'

'Yes, my dear. Back at the embassy. On British soil we can do what we would do in Britain. I have quite the selection of fine gins, if you like that sort of thing.' I will admit that I was tempted but the handsy ambassador was most likely just trying to get me into the back of his car for another feel and I was going to punch him on the nose if he tried again.

'No, thank you, Lord Edgar. I think I will call it a night.' When he gave a small nod of disappointed acceptance, I added, 'If you can think of anything that you can do, any strings you might be able to pull to get my friends out of this mess, I will be very grateful.' I touched his arm to reinforce the suggestion of what grateful could mean. Not that I had any intention of following through in the way he so clearly wanted, but I thought it was a good idea to motivate the man.

He grinned at me and growled like a tiger again, this time clawing the air with mock paws. He was trying to be saucy or sexy or something, but he just looked like an idiot. 'I shall do my best, my lovely filly.' I turned to go but jumped when Jermaine startled me by darting swiftly behind me. I spun around to find his hand gripping the ambassador's arm – he had been about to smack my bum!

Jermaine released his grip, saying, 'None of that now, sir. There's a good gentleman.' Lord Edgar rubbed his arm where Jermaine had grabbed it but didn't complain. Jared appeared at his side though, belatedly stepping in to protect his principle. He had to look up to lock eyes with Jermaine but managed to do so with a healthy amount of threat.

'That's enough now, Jared,' laughed the ambassador. 'It's all in good sport.' He nodded his head at me. 'Goodnight, Mrs Fisher. I will see you on the morrow.' Then he departed, Jared following after one last hard stare at my butler.

I rolled my eyes at the show of machismo, then spoke to Martin and Deepa. 'I'm calling it a night. The coronation is bound to be quite something tomorrow, so I want some sleep. It has been quite the day.'

'What about Rick and Akamu?' asked Deepa. 'Will they be allowed to travel with us when we leave?

I pursed my lips and shrugged my shoulders. 'I don't know.' I genuinely didn't.

They decided my policy of getting to bed was almost certainly the right one so the four of us took a slow walk back to our rooms. The sky outside was filled with a billion stars, all twinkling, and the moon was full and high, casting glowing, milky light to illuminate the gardens and water features outside. It was a beautiful place to be; if only I wasn't certain that I was being lied to, I might have been able to enjoy it.

A Really Unwelcome Intruder

Jermaine escorted me to my door and then bid me a good night before returning to his suite next door. His valet was still there waiting for him which reminded me that Aladdin had been gone for some hours now and no one had attempted to replace him. It suited me; I was happy to be alone. I had my attack dog after all. Anna arrived at a run when she heard the door open, tried to get out once more and barked her frustration when I stopped her. The bark was heard by the Corgis who took to howling again.

I slammed the door shut with a shove from my hip and thought about trying to have a conversation with Anna about boys. I held her in front on my face as I tried to frame what I wanted to say. She licked my nose and panted with excitement, then one of the Corgis howled again, the noise reaching her ears and she wriggled to be set free again.

With a sigh, I put her down so she could scratch at the door and went to my bedroom to get changed. Once I had stripped off the traditional outfit and changed into my flannel pyjamas, I settled Anna in her bed right next to mine and closed the bedroom door so she couldn't spend the night scratching at the front door. Then, I pulled back the covers to get in but decided I might want water in the night. If I had a valet, this sort of need would be taken care of, but because I kicked Aladdin out, I was going to have to find a glass for myself. Water was easy enough; there was a stocked refrigerator, however I couldn't find a cup or a glass of anything better than a flower vase to put it in.

Accepting defeat, I started back to my bedroom, stubbing my toe on the corner of a low table in the dark and unfamiliar room. I winced and said several choice words, but as I ducked my head to inspect the damage, a blade swished through the air above me. Had I not bent down at that precise moment, it would have taken my head clean off.

69

The man holding it had put everything into the swing, so having connected with thin air he lost his balance, pitched to the side and almost fell over. I screamed, forgetting the pain in my foot as I ran away. His loss of balance gave me a brief head start but I was alone in the suite and I had no weapon I could use to defend myself.

The man yelled a blood-curdling war cry as he chased after me, brandishing the curved sword so I could see it each time I glanced behind me. In the dark room, I couldn't see him very well, but he was dressed like one of the royal guards in black and white but was far smaller than most of the guards I had seen thus far. I could tell because the uniform hung off him. I wasn't paying much attention to detail though, I was trying to get away, moonlight coming through the window glinted off the sword to give me a rough idea where he was as I fled.

I had been near the servant's room when I stubbed my toe. It was at the far end of the suite and as far from the front door and the small chance of escape it might offer as possible. That was where I had to go, but I was half hopping from my stubbed toes and unlikely to outrun him. Instead, I started throwing objects behind me as I passed them. A vase. A table lamp. I yanked a curtain closed as I ran along a passage and heard him shred it with the sword. It didn't hold him up for long, but it bought me another second.

Then I came into the main living area, a wide space with huge panoramic windows looking out over the gardens and the city beyond the palace wall. It was filled with couches and tables, large objet d'art pieces and hunks of gold formed into candlesticks and ornaments. The passageway to the lobby and the chance of escape was through the door on the far side of the room. My running hobble wasn't as fast as it needed to be though, he was catching up and I could tell I wouldn't make it to the door before he caught me.

70

To accentuate that point, a knife flew past me to bury itself an inch deep in the wood of the door. I squealed again and threw myself over a couch, grabbing two cushions as I went.

With the option of running away now lost, I turned to face him. 'What do you want? Who sent you?' I demanded. He grinned and laughed, swishing his sword in a large figure eight as he slowly advanced. He thought this was over; I had nowhere left to run and no way to fight him off. Anna was barking like mad, but I had shut the bedroom door when I left it to stop her following me; in the dark she has a habit of getting under my feet. I could do with her aggression right now, but the man would most likely skewer her, so I was glad she was locked away.

He came closer, going slow to savour the moment. I looked at the daft cushions in my hands and threw them at him. They had about as much effect as you might imagine. Then I heard the click of my front door opening and my heart raced even harder than it had been. Jermaine was coming to rescue me!

The man with the sword heard the door too, his smile dropping as he gritted his teeth. Then he pointed the tip of the sword at me, keeping me in place as he moved around, getting in position to attack whoever was coming in.

In terror, I yelled, 'Watch out, Jermaine!'

My attacker couldn't be two places at once, so as his attention left me and he dismissed me as the lesser concern, I moved. My plan was to distract him and split his attention; make him look at me to give Jermaine an opening for his own attack. I had seen Jermaine in action several times so my confidence of surviving this encounter had gone from almost zero to very high in a heartbeat.

'Hello? Am I interrupting something?' asked Lord Edgar.

It wasn't Jermaine at all! It was the daft and horny British ambassador back to try his luck again. He was still in the stateroom's lobby, his hesitation prolonging his life as the man with the sword was ready to strike as soon as anyone came through the door into the living room.

It wasn't bravery driving me, it was just survival instinct. The only weapons I had were cushions. Maybe they would do though. The first one bounced off Mustafa the Murderer's head, drawing his attention just before Lord Edgar stuck his head through the door.

It gave my fellow Brit the chance to see the sword-swinging maniac, a single glance telling him what was happening. Any hope that he might come to my rescue got dashed instantly because he screamed like a little girl on a roller coaster and fainted.

Now I had to save him too.

I shouted, 'Hey!' just before I threw the next cushion. It too just bounced off, this time striking him squarely in the face, but it did the job of blinding him so he couldn't see me running full tilt across the room in a silent charge.

He batted the cushion across the room with his free hand before I could get to him which left me skidding to a halt right in front of him with nothing but a cushion in my right hand. He laughed. He actually laughed. Then dropped the sword to his side and motioned for me to give it my best shot. He even turned his chin upwards to give me a better angle.

So I hit him. I gave the swing everything I had and whacked him in the side of his amused face with the cushion. You might think it would have been more sporting to tell him about the gold candlesticks I had quickly zipped inside the case, but what would have been the fun in that?

His head snapped back from the impact, came back to level with a curious expression plastered on his face and then the sword clattered to the floor as his eyes rolled backward. He didn't fall over like a felled tree, he more sort of collapsed inward on himself like Obi-Wan Kenobi when Darth Vader cut him down in Star Wars.

I raised the cushion for a second strike, but the first one had done the trick. It had also ripped the fabric of the cushion which allowed one of the candlesticks to fall out. It hit my foot, the one that I hadn't stubbed on an unseen object in the dark and made stars dance in front of my eyes as I too fell to the floor with more choice words spilling from my lips.

'Goodness,' said the ambassador. 'That was some colourful language.'

Rubbing my aching toes, I asked, 'Are you alright, Lord Edgar?' I couldn't find the energy to be embarrassed about my choice of expletives; my feet hurt too much.

'Yes, my dear. I fear I may have fainted just then. Your friend gave me quite the fright. Is he dead?'

My breath froze and my heart stopped beating as I stared at the fallen form. Then I saw his chest rise and let go the fear that I might have killed him. 'No, but he is out for now. We need to tie him up before he comes around.'

'Goodness. Surely, we should just call security? They will deal with him.'

Despite the throbbing in my feet, I stood up, forcing myself to accept the pain and get moving. I found a light switch. 'He is security,' I pointed out, showing Lord Edgar the man's clothing. 'I think he might be one of the Maharaja's personal guards.' Then something else occurred to me. 'Hold on. How did you get into my room?'

With the light on, I could see his cheeks colour. 'Oh, I ah… bribed a guard to let me in.' I really wanted to ask what he thought might happen once he snuck into my stateroom, but he spoke before I could. 'I have news of your friends,' he smiled knowingly. 'I was able to make some calls, call in some favours and get them a stay of execution, so to speak. I came to collect on your promise.'

Yet again I rolled my eyes. 'Okay, one, I didn't make a promise. Two, what exactly does a stay of execution mean and three, are you kidding me? You break into my room hoping to bed me? You're like some creepy, well-spoken rapist, you know that?'

He looked crestfallen. 'I rather hoped I might come off as more like David Niven, sexy cat burglar and all-around scoundrel the ladies cannot resist.'

I narrowed my eyes at him. 'Well, you failed. Miserably. Now make yourself useful and help me tie Mustafa the Murderer up.' I needed to call him something and it was the first name that came to me. 'I need to alert my friends and find out who is behind whatever the heck is going on here.'

While I looked around for something to use as rope, he said, 'You can come with me to the British embassy still. I can keep you safe there.'

I found some ornate hold back thingies for the curtains that would do the trick. I just needed to cut it. Feeling quite put upon as I picked up the sword to hack at the curtains, I replied, 'I am the only British member of the group. We are truly multi-national so going with you isn't an option.'

'I can arrange for cars to get you to the airport. You and your friends can at least escape before anything else happens.'

'Not without Rick and Akamu. My two friends are wrongfully imprisoned and likely to be punished for a crime they didn't commit. I am going nowhere without them.'

He didn't voice an argument, choosing instead to not lend a hand either as he watched with fascination while I pulled the hold back apart to make lengths of rope. Mustafa the Murderer had a strong pulse and I doubted the cut to his chin and lump on his cheek were life threatening so I wasn't very gentle as I rolled him over and yanked his arms back. It was heavy work though, the man weighing far more than me. 'Can you help?' I snapped, frustrated.

It jolted the dignitary into action finally. 'Goodness, yes. Sorry.' As he knelt next to me and grabbed both arms so I could tie them, he said, 'You seem very adept at this.'

I felt like muttering about how life had prepared me recently. Instead I asked, 'You said you had news about my friends?'

'Oh, yes. The stay of execution. I was able to give them an additional twenty-four hours before their flogging will take place.' He shot me a grin that announced how impressed he was with himself.

I think he was waiting for me to tell him how impressed I was, so his smile crashed to the tile when I curled my lip in disgust. 'That's it? An extra day but they get flogged anyway?'

'I... I...' he stuttered.

I snapped, 'Grab his feet.' Lord Edgar complied, which allowed me to loop the rope around his feet and back up to his hands, pulling his ankles up so they almost touched his hands. Mustafa was now shaped like a banana only bent backward.

Anna barked again. She had fallen quiet, undoubtedly listening and trying to work out what was going on, but she wanted out of the bedroom. Satisfied that Mustafa was secure, I pushed myself off the floor and set her free. As expected, she shot out of the room, took one look at the ambassador and started barking at him as she burst into an attack sprint.

His eyes flared in terror and he started to back away, but my shout brought her to a skidding stop. I had been working on behaviour with her, trying to instil some sense of right and wrong, manners, and obedience. It wasn't going very well but I had managed to curb her habit of ankle biting. Not that she was happy about it and she looked grumpy now as she left Lord Edgar alone and nudged Mustafa with her nose.

So, what now? I asked myself. I had no idea who I could trust in the palace. Was the Maharaja himself behind this? Or his uncle? Or the creepy general? How about the vizier? At this point in time the only ones I could trust were the friends I had brought with me and probably the ambassador with the over-active libido.

I needed to alert Jermaine, but then I remembered how both Rick and Akamu's valets had claimed they went out looking for alcohol and wondered if any of us could trust the men in our rooms. Aladdin had tried to warn me something was going on. I wish I had the ability to contact him because I wanted to know more now. Whatever else I did, I wanted Jermaine with me.

'Come on, Anna. We need to fetch Jermaine.' I was still in my pyjamas but that didn't matter, I was going to knock on his door and wake him or wake his valet.

It was then that I realised Anna was missing. 'Anna?' A moment ago she had been licking Mustafa's nose, entertaining herself by bothering the unresponsive human. Now she was nowhere to be seen.

'She wandered off that way,' said Lord Edgar, pointing toward the back of the suite. Muttering to myself, I followed, going back the way I fled when Mustafa tried to kill me. Then it struck me: what was he doing at the back end of my suite? He would have come in through the front door. Even if he had come in over the balcony and through the door there, which he hadn't because it was still shut, he would have been in the middle of the suite, but he was all the way in the back. Had he been looking for something?

The answer presented itself as soon as I looked for it.

Secret Passage

There was an opening in the back of my suite, a door hidden behind a bookcase. It was such a ridiculous cliché that I couldn't help but laugh. Unfortunately, I was fairly certain my missing dog had already found it and decided to explore.

At least I now knew how Mustafa got into my suite. 'Lord Edgar,' I called.

'Yes, dear?' he said from about an inch behind me, startling me and making me spin around to slap his arm in fright.

'Don't sneak up on me, dammit.' My poor heart couldn't take much more excitement this evening. The ambassador wasn't listening though, he was distracted by my chest as it heaved from my intake of breath. 'Do you mind?' I asked, bringing his eyes back up to mine.

He tried a lopsided grin. 'You know you cut quite the enticing figure, even in those pyjamas...'

'No,' I cut him off before he could finish his sentence. 'I think my dog went in there,' I said pointing to the hole behind the bookcase. 'I need to find her, but I also want to see where it goes. You're coming with me.'

'I am?'

'Yes. They might think twice about killing you. We need to be quiet though. Stealthy. Can you do that?' He mimed zipping his mouth shut and locking it and then throwing away the key. 'Super. Wait here.'

'Where are y...'

'Ah!' I chided, my finger raised to remind him of his vow of silence. I needed Anna's lead, a pair of shoes and my phone so I could call Jermaine and use it as a torch if necessary. Lord Edgar stayed by the secret passage as I fetched things from my bedroom, then, with a steely sense of determination, I went into the dark passage.

It was cold inside, far cooler than my room which was a balmy, pleasant temperature. The passageway was formed of solid stone, a little more than six feet high and about three feet across. There was no lighting at all, so reluctantly, because it would announce my presence to anyone further down the passageway, I turned on the light on my phone.

I swung it both ways. The passageway ended a few feet further along to the left, so my only option was right. I set off, the ambassador on my shoulder and called Jermaine as I crept along in the dark.

I got no answer, the call frustratingly going to his answer service before I thumbed the cancel button. I wasn't going to need it though, fifty yards along the passageway, we reached a recess in the wall to my right and a lever set into a wooden panel I was willing to bet was the back of another bookcase.

'This is all very exciting,' whispered Lord Edgar. 'I feel like one of the forty thieves.' I wasn't sure exciting was the word I would use. Terrifying would be a better fit for how I was feeling. Nevertheless, I grabbed the lever and yanked it upward. Something clicked, and the wooden panel moved inward a half inch, hinging from the righthand edge to swing open as I pushed it.

I was sure from the distance we had walked that this must be Jermaine's suite, but I crept cautiously anyway in case he too had suffered an intruder. He hadn't though and was sleeping in his bed with one arm and a leg hanging out and a small teddy bear tucked in next to his head. The teddy bear had on a tuxedo. I vowed to ask him about Mr Bear when the time was right; this wasn't it though, so I let it go and placed a gentle hand on his shoulder to wake him.

My sleeping butler came to full alertness in a nanosecond, spinning around to grab my wrist with one hand as the other pulled back to deliver a strike. Lord Edgar squealed in fright which was probably what saved me from getting whacked in the head.

'Madam! You gave me such a fright,' exclaimed Jermaine as he let me go and flicked on his bedside light.

'I gave you a fright?' This time my heart was threatening to tear loose of its mooring and sail away. I genuinely feared that I might have a heart attack if the constant shocks persisted. With a hand to my chest, I sat on his bed so I wouldn't fall down. I didn't have time for this though. 'Jermaine, sweetie, there's another intruder in my room.'

'Another snake?'

'No, one of the Maharaja's personal guards. He used a secret passage to get in and brought a sword with him.'

'It's all very cloak and dagger, isn't it?' Lord Edgar enthused.

Jermaine looked like he had a ton of questions, but he didn't ask any of them. He acted instead, sliding across to the other side of his bed to find his clothes. As he stood up to slip his own silk pyjama bottoms on, I realised that he was naked and turned my embarrassed face away.

I had just seen my butler's muscular bum!

To cover my flusterment, I said, 'Anna is missing in the passageway. I need to find her.'

80

'What about the man in your room?' Jermaine asked as he cinched a robe around his waist and slipped on a pair of house slippers.

My answer paused on my lips as I looked at him again. Somehow he looked like a butler again – like if I were to describe what a nineteenth century butler wore in his bedroom, this would be it. The tall Jamaican had on silk pyjamas, a cotton bath gown and a pair of leather house slippers. To top the outfit off, he collected the small bear in the tuxedo and tucked it into the left breast pocket on his robe so it could look out and see what was happening. I shook my head to break the train of thought. 'We, ah... we tied him up. He's going nowhere. My first priority is to find Anna, and I am hoping the passage will lead to somewhere that might tell me what is going on or who is behind all this.'

'We seem to have found ourselves in hot water again, madam.' I couldn't argue with that. I looked at Lord Edgar, making sure he was still up for this, but he just mimed keeping his mouth shut again with a smile.

Back in the secret passageway, Jermaine checked left and right, glanced at me and led the way when I indicated a direction. I really wanted to shout for Anna to come back, but it felt safer not to. She had lived with Japanese criminals for most of her life and had killed a cobra this afternoon; I was fairly sure she would be able to handle whatever she found ahead. I wasn't so sure I could.

Another fifty yards further on, we found another wooden panel and another lever. This time it would be Barbie's stateroom. A single exchanged glance between Jermaine and I confirmed that we both wanted to check she was alright.

The bookcase opened just like the last one, allowing us to spill into her stateroom. They were all laid out the same so even in the dark we knew where the master bedroom was and where we needed to go to find her.

With so little background noise, we all heard her the moment we came through the doorway. Sharp cries rang out, unmistakably her voice – we were too late!

Jermaine went through the door ahead of me, tensed as he heard his friend being murdered and I only just caught hold of his arm before he broke into a run. My hand hooked around his elbow stopped him, but I had to grab on with both hands as he tried to break free. 'Madam!' he insisted in a hushed breath. 'I have to save her!'

I placed a finger to my lips, then whispered, 'She doesn't need saving.'

'Madam?' Then he heard it too. Barbie wasn't being murdered. Quite the opposite in fact and the squeals I thought were from pain were also quite the opposite. His eyes locked with mine in the dark, both of us silently agreeing that we should leave Barbie and Hideki alone for the time being. It would have been quite the *oops* moment if we had burst into her bedroom to save her.

Dungeons

Back in the passage we agreed that we would leave Martin and Deepa alone as well. Not that I thought they were also getting busy but creeping about in secret passageways wasn't a thing we needed to do as a group activity.

'Lord Edgar, perhaps it would be prudent for you to let us continue without you,' I suggested before we set off again. I dragged him along initially because I didn't want to go into the dark, scary passageway by myself. With Jermaine at my side I felt far safer and the British ambassador wasn't going to be of much use unless I needed someone to do my screaming for me.

He wasn't about to be benched though. 'Nonsense, Mrs Fisher. This evening calls for some true Dunkirk spirit, wot? You shall not find me wanting. Besides, how else am I to prove my worth and win your heart?'

I rolled my eyes, the act going unseen in the poorly lit passageway. Jermaine checked I was ready to move and started walking, making almost no noise with his slippered feet. The passageway went on in a straight line for another hundred yards before we reached a corner. Jermaine strode around it before I could question if it was safe, but the sound of claws skittering over the stone floor propelled me forward.

Little Anna was wagging her tail like mad and bouncing onto her hind legs to stand like a meercat at my feet. I scooped her up. 'Mummy was worried, Anna. You shouldn't wander off like that.' I got a lick to my chin in response.

Jermaine reappeared from the gloom ahead. 'Madam there are stairs here. Do you wish to return to your rooms or press on? I will remain with you regardless of your decision.'

'And I as well,' chimed Lord Edgar though his company filled me with neither joy nor a sense of security. Mostly I got the sense that he was undressing me with his eyes the whole time.

I did want to return to my rooms. I wanted to go back there and pack and run away but I couldn't, so despite having no wish to press on, that was exactly what I did. 'Let's see where it leads.'

I slipped around Jermaine, keeping Anna tucked under my arm as I found the stairs and started to descend. It was a narrow spiral staircase, the steps so small I felt I needed to keep one hand on the wall the whole time. It went down and down, around and around so many times that I soon lost track of how many full circles we had made or how far down we might have descended. My brain told me we must be well below ground though. After several minutes, light started to appear ahead – wherever we were going was lit.

Blinking in the sudden light, I emerged into a new passageway, this one far larger, higher and wider with arched supports to hold the palace above it. This time the passageway stretched in both directions, giving an unwelcome option of which way to go. Either could lead to danger though neither was likely to provide salvation. Jermaine was paused and waiting my next instruction. When I glanced at Lord Edgar, he mimed keeping his lips shut again.

I twitched my nose; being down here felt unwise. If we ran into anyone, it would be someone involved in the plot to kill me, if that was what was going on, and that meant we needed to be very careful. 'Let's just have a quick nose around, see what we find and get back to your suite.'

'My suite?' asked Jermaine.

84

'Yes. I'm not sleeping in mine. No one tried to kill you yet, so maybe it is just me they are after. I'll stay with you in your suite and maybe that will throw them off. In the morning we need to come up with a better plan for survival.'

'Very good, madam.'

I chose to go right for no reason at all, keeping my footsteps quiet; the need for stealth greater now than before. After two steps I paused, causing Jermaine to almost bump into me. 'We need to mark our route. There might be lots of turns ahead so we should mark each intersection.'

'Brilliant,' murmured Lord Edgar.

It was hardly brilliant. Hansel and Gretel managed to think of it a few centuries ago. Jermaine found a handy piece of stone on the floor and used it to mark the staircase with an up arrow. Then at the first corner, he marked the walls to show we needed to turn there to get back to the stairs. Behind Jermaine and me, as we walked down the centre of the passageway, Lord Edgar was sidling along the wall, keeping to the shadows as much as possible and glancing about constantly in an act of vigilance. He looked like an idiot again, this time doing a poor impression of James Bond.

The passageway reached a T junction, but I wasn't stifled by the choice of left and right this time, I was stunned by the bars I could see on a dozen doors. It was a dungeon!

Jermaine saw it too. I looked in both directions, but there was no one about. There was a hand sticking out between some bars though, the sight shocking me and making my feet move. I crossed the floor, Jermaine right by me but my very brief hope that the hand might belong to Rick or Akamu was soon dashed when I saw the face of the man through the bars.

It was Aladdin!

He was either asleep or unconscious, but when I touched his skin, he jerked awake, turning his face so I could see the side which had been hidden in shadow: it was badly bruised, his right eye almost swollen shut.

'Oh, my goodness. Aladdin what happened?'

He gripped my hands through the bars. 'They grabbed me right after I left your stateroom. They knew all about what I had told you; I think your rooms might be bugged.'

'They are most likely all bugged then,' said Jermaine. 'Are you badly injured, sir?'

Aladdin shook his head. 'No. It is superficial; nothing broken but I doubt they plan to let me survive. Can you get me out?' Jermaine went in search of keys, taking Lord Edgar with him, which left me crouching at the bars of the dungeon. Anna wriggled to be put down, so I plopped her on the cold floor and watched as she slid between the bars to explore.

Watching her, Aladdin said, 'If only it were that easy.'

I squeezed his hand. 'Who did this?'

He winced as he shifted position. 'Some of the Maharaja's personal guards. They didn't tell me why and didn't ask me any questions other than what I knew. They wanted me to tell them why I thought the Maharaja had been replaced.'

'What did you say?'

'I told them the same thing I told you: I have been his valet since birth until just a short while ago. I believe that I know him better than his mother or father ever did and the boy sitting on the throne is not the same person. I travelled with him to America last year when he insisted he needed to go and I watched as he was influenced by their culture. He talked about sweeping reforms when he became the Maharaja, about a new Zangrabar that he would lead into the twenty-first century. When he returned here a few weeks ago after the sapphire was found, it was all he could talk about. How we could revolutionise the medical services to give care for those without the means to pay for it themselves, how we could empower women to be better educated and hold jobs as lawyers or doctors instead of cleaning ladies and cooks. Then, six days ago he stopped talking about any of it and that is because they replaced him. I don't know how, but that is what I know and that is what I told them. They asked who else I had spoken to then threw me in here. They haven't come back since.'

'Who else have you told?'

'No one. That was when I got the beating. They didn't believe me, so they did their best to persuade the truth from me. They are fools though; if I had a name to give them, I would take it to my grave.'

I scanned around for any sign of Jermaine or Lord Edgar. They had vanished in search of the keys, though there was no reason to believe they would be down here. I doubted they would be hung on a convenient hook around the corner but on top of rescuing Rick and Akamu, I now had my palace valet to free.

'Aladdin, two of my friends, the older gentlemen in my party, went missing earlier this evening. Their valets reported that they went to the docks to look for booze. I think they were lying. Why would they do that?'

Aladdin mimed spitting in his disgust. 'Fariq and Akari? Those two are the sons of an illegitimate goat. Whoever is behind this will have employed them to play along. You can bet they were lying; it is as natural as eating hummus to them.'

'Who did you think is behind this?' I wanted to ask the question the moment we found him, but I had been working up to it and making sure I showed concern for him before wringing him for answers. But since he introduced the subject...

He waved a frustrated arm in the air in response. 'I have no idea. If I am right and the boy you met as the Maharaja tonight is indeed a fake, then I would have to ask who stands to gain.'

'That's right,' I replied, astonished that someone else thought to ask what I always felt was the most pertinent and obvious question. 'Who stands to gain? The fake Maharaja does, but I cannot see how a teenage boy could manipulate his way into replacing the genuine Maharaja without a lot of help.'

'And that is why I am now locked in a dungeon. It could be that everyone in the palace is in on this except me. I didn't know who I could trust, which is why I approached you. Even that wasn't a safe move though.' He sighed and winced again as he shifted position once more. Anna got bored with sniffing around the dust and dirt in the ancient cell but figured the man on the floor probably wanted to give her some affection so climbed onto his lap without invite. He gave her an absentminded pat.

If he had anything else to say, it was forgotten as Jermaine and Lord Edgar reappeared with a bunch of keys. 'I found these,' Jermaine announced, holding them up for me to see. It was a large bunch on a ring one could put an arm through. The keys were massive too, designed to fit exactly the kind of lock on the ancient cell door.

I stood up and dusted myself off a bit, then while Jermaine tried the keys one at a time, I wandered down the line of cells to see if there were any other occupants. Secretly I prayed I wouldn't find a skeleton chained to a wall in any of them. I didn't but I did note that there were only six cells and there looked to be at least a dozen keys on the bunch Jermaine found.

'Jermaine, how many keys have you got there?'

He paused in his efforts to open the door while he quickly counted. 'Twelve, madam.'

'Aladdin are there any more cells in this dungeon?'

Aladdin blinked at me. 'I couldn't say, Mrs Fisher. I didn't even know there was a dungeon beneath the palace, and I have worked here all my adult life.' I thought about that for a second and logged the information for later. He arrived at the same conclusion though, 'You think the real Maharaja might be down here in another cell?'

I pursed my lips before I answered. I still wasn't convinced that the Maharaja wasn't the real Maharaja. Yes, he was an annoying teenage boy with a convincing American accent and not even slightly like the ruler of a rich nation I expected to meet. How would you find a replacement lookalike though? How would you switch one for the other and convince all the people around you? It was just too far-fetched. Nevertheless, there was something going on and thus far it was the only explanation I had.

What I said was. 'I think we should explore.'

Jermaine was still trying keys, Aladdin standing just inside the cell in readiness to depart, but Jermaine must have been through the bunch more than twice by now. 'The key for this cell isn't here, madam.'

'Are you sure?' asked Aladdin, clearly keen to leave the confined space.

A noise echoing along the passageway snapped all our heads around to stare in the same direction: someone was coming. 'Madam, we need to leave,' said Jermaine, scooping Anna before she could start running and covering her mouth with a giant hand before she could begin barking. Lord Edgar looked about with panicked eyes, suddenly worried he might be caught in a diplomatically embarrassing situation on account of his determination to get into my knickers. He didn't bother to wait for me or Jermaine, he simply turned and ran back toward the stairs and salvation.

'Wait,' Aladdin pleaded, his voice hushed but desperate. 'Don't leave me here!'

I felt bad about it but getting caught would just result in Jermaine and me becoming Aladdin's cell mates. Or worse. 'Sorry.' I looked at him with real sorrow. 'Look, we know where you are and how to find you. Give me some time. We'll come back for you, I promise.'

He grabbed my hand before I could move away and held it tight as he spoke, 'You have to stop the coronation. Whatever else happens, you have to prevent the fake Maharaja from being crowned. Promise me that,' he demanded. 'Don't worry about me but swear on the souls of your ancestors that you will find the real Maharaja and save him.'

The voices around the corner were getting closer and we had to go, or it wouldn't matter what I promised. 'Okay. I promise, Aladdin. Now sit tight, we will be back for you.'

The moment Aladdin released my hand, Jermaine yanked me across the passageway and out of sight back toward the spiral stairs. I didn't get to see who was coming, which was a shame. I wanted to see if the person coming was who I thought it might be. In order to see them though, I would have to let them see me and that would get me killed most likely.

So instead, just like always, I was going to have to work it all out the hard way.

There were no more stairs on the way up than there had been on the way down, but my thighs were protesting by the time I got back to the top. Barbie would be impressed that I did them all without a break, telling myself to just keep moving and embrace the calorie burn. In the passageway at the top once more, I rested a few seconds just because I felt dizzy and disorientated from doing so many circles.

The ambassador was not so fit or determined and was a few years older than me. I passed him easily about halfway up, then left him behind to wait for him at the top. 'Goodness,' he puffed as his head came into sight. 'That is a lot of steps. I probably shouldn't have had so much chocolate this evening.'

'We need to wake the others,' I said rather breathlessly as I forced myself to move on, once again leaving Lord Edgar behind. 'We're all in trouble, I think.'

Jermaine reached the first wooden panel and lever, behind which we should find Martin Baker. 'Very good, madam. Shall we gather in one room?'

I nodded at his suggestion. 'I think we should. I need some items from my room though, I don't intend to stay in pyjamas all night.'

'I should come with you.'

I waved him off. 'Gather everyone together and then fetch me. Use this passageway to move about in case they are watching the front doors.'

'What about the guard you tied up?' asked Lord Edgar, reminding me that he was still with us.

Quickly I said, 'Jermaine, you go. I'll meet you in Rick's room. No one will think to look there, and I expect his valet to be elsewhere since Rick is in jail.' Then I grabbed the ambassador's arm and dragged him with me toward the secret entrance back into my own suite. 'Lord Edgar, what are you still doing with us?' He looked confused by the question. 'I mean, why are you still hanging around? You have no stake in this misadventure but could cause yourself all sorts of bother if you get caught.'

He straightened his bow tie as we came into my suite and shot me a look that was most likely supposed to be steely determination but mostly looked like he needed to use the smallest room. Then he said, 'Babe...'

'Babe?' I squinted at him.

He tried again, but the steely determination was already failing. 'Patricia?' he tried nervously. I nodded that he could continue. 'Patricia, I am given to understand that exciting and dangerous experiences can cause heightened libido in those persons engaged in the life-threateni...'

'No.'

'But...'

'No.'

'You don't know what I was going to say,' he whined.

'Just no. Okay?' When he looked like he might argue again, I added, 'You were going to suggest we have sex since we are both so turned on by the action and adventure this evening and that given the danger we find ourselves in it might be our last chance before we get killed. Is that about right?'

'Um.'

93

'Thought so. Now make yourself useful and check on Mustafa the Murderer while I get changed and pack a few things.' I turned to go to my bedroom but reran the conversation in my head and stopped so I could make one final point clear. 'Me telling you that I am getting changed is not an indication that I want you to accidentally,' I did quote fingers, 'find me naked. Is that clear?'

'Perfectly, Patricia. Um, who is Mustafa?'

I rolled my eyes. 'The thug we tied up. I have no idea what his name is and I have to call him something. Trust me, there will be more thugs to deal with yet and it gets confusing if you don't know which one someone is talking about.' I left him to the task and stomped off to the master bedroom, Anna dancing along at my feet because she thought it was biscuit time. I barely noticed her because I was wondering when it was that I had become a man magnet. Until the age of fifty-three I had slept with only one man; the man I married. Now the count had increased to two with Alistair and I was very glad about it, but in the recent weeks several men had propositioned me and though I had dropped a few pounds and more than a dress size, I was surprised by the attention.

I didn't hang about getting changed, choosing jeans and a sweater, then putting my running shoes back on because they were comfortable. I made sure Anna had a drink of water and gave her a biscuit, then slipped my messenger handbag over one shoulder and went to see what Lord Edgar was doing.

He was outside my door looking sheepish and holding some ropes. Mustafa had escaped!

I took the ropes from him. They had been cut, but Mustafa didn't have a knife with him and should not have been able to get up to find one in the suite. 'Were these where we left him?' I asked.

'Yes.'

'Then someone cut him free. Either way, they know their attempt to kill me failed and are more likely to be watching to see what we do.'

'What are we going to do?'

'Research,' I declared, whistling for Anna to follow as once again I walked to the far end of my suite and back to the secret passage.

The wooden panel leading to Rick's room was open, I could see the light from within shining out of it. Jermaine came out of it looking for me before I got there, silently expressing his concern for my wellbeing with his impatience.

'Do we have everyone?' I asked as I passed him.

'Yes, madam. They are all in the main living area. Lieutenant Baker swept for bugs already and found seventeen. He has disabled the ones in the main living area and manoeuvred a lamp in front of a camera he found. May I bring you a coffee?' It was so typical for Jermaine to provide refreshments.

I said, 'Thank you, yes,' as I made my way through the stateroom. Behind me he asked Lord Edgar the same question then butlered off to fetch our drinks as I found everyone else. As they sleepily greeted me, I indicated the extra man. 'I don't think you have met Lord Edgar. He is the British ambassador to Zangrabar.' For his benefit, I introduced each of the other people present and explained who they were.

Barbie was the first of my friends to speak. 'Jermaine said the situation with Rick and Akamu is worse than we thought?'

Grasping one hand with the other, I circled the room a little, fret causing my feet to feel agitated. 'That is one way to put it. The Zangrabar punishment for public inebriation is public flogging.' Barbie's hand shot to her mouth but everyones' eyes flared wide in shock at the news. 'That will happen in two days' time, but it is not the real news I need to share with you.'

Martin Baker's brow furrowed. 'Then what is? Or do I really just not want to know?' I cocked my head at his question: he probably didn't want to know. Unfortunately, he had to, as did everyone else.

'I believe we have walked into some kind of plot to usurp rule in Zangrabar or overthrow the crown or something. My valet, Aladdin, the one that met us at the airport with the general confided in me today. As soon as the door to my suite was shut, he claimed the Maharaja we met is a fake.' My friends' faces were lined with disbelief at what I was telling them, but I was barely getting started. I went on to tell them about Rick and Akamu's valets, their supposed excursion in ceremonial dress and then Mustafa the Murderer, the secret passages, the snake and finding Aladdin in the dungeons.

By the time I was finished, I felt that I needed a lie down. We were in it really deep this time.

Deepa had a question. 'If the stuff about the Maharaja being fake and the plot to overthrow the crown or whatever is true, I still don't see why they would grab Rick and Akamu or why they would try to kill you.'

She had me there. 'I'm not sure either. But if Aladdin is right then we have to assume I was talking to the fake Maharaja this evening and I revealed to him my concern that something was amiss here. Given that I was invited solely for solving the mystery of the sapphire, it stands to reason that they think I might poke about and do some investigating here too. Having shown them my hand, they decided it would be easier to just kill me.'

'Didn't the snake come before you spoke with them this evening?' asked Martin.

'Yes, it did, but it was after Aladdin confided in me, so they knew I had heard the truth, if that's what it is. You found how many listening devices

97

and cameras in this suite? They have heard every word everyone of us has said since we arrived up until this point.

Barbie shot Hideki a sideways look and sniggered behind her hands, her eyes twinkling in embarrassed delight. No one else saw it, but Hideki saw me and knew that I knew what had caused Barbie's chuckle. He covered his own embarrassment with a question. 'So what do we do now? What are our options?'

Somehow, despite having no qualifications, I was the leader of this group and they were looking to me for guidance. I let myself fall backward onto a couch, my body weary from the day and still bruised from being thrown about on the plane. Anna jumped up next to me and cuddled into my left hip. 'Our options are limited,' I said before anyone could prompt me. 'We have no back up and even if we all escape the palace and hide in our respective embassies, we are still left with Rick and Akamu facing a kangaroo court and there is no US embassy here so Barbie has nowhere to go. Anyone that wants to get to safety should go but I am staying. I cannot tell anyone at the palace about the fake Maharaja though because I have not the first idea who might be involved.' Then I told them about the number of keys against the number of cells we found and the possibility that the true Maharaja might still be in the palace waiting to be rescued.

Jermaine summed it up neatly. 'In order for us to solve this mystery, rescue Mr Hutton and Mr Kameāloha and walk away unscathed, we have to find out what is going on, find out who is behind whatever is going on and then stop them while simultaneously freeing the true Maharaja and overpowering the Maharaja that everyone thinks is the real one.'

Martin blew out a breath. 'Easy then. What shall we do after that?'

Deepa placed a hand of reassurance on his forearm. 'We can work this out together. Isn't that right, Mrs Fisher?'

Barbie looked at me, her perma-smile absent for once. 'Is it research time?'

Phones, tablets, and a laptop were brought into use as the team each started to work in singles or pairs on different elements of the mystery. Lord Edgar wanted to help but had no idea how to, so chipped in by making more coffee, waving his arm at Jermaine when my butler attempted to stop his research project to perform the mundane task instead. I'll say this for Lord Edgar; if this evening was all about getting me into bed, then he got an A for effort. Achievement was going to be an F but well done for trying.

Barbie and Deepa were working on the military aspect, delving into enemies of Zangrabar, past conflicts and who might wish to shoot down the Maharaja's private jet. While they did that and looked for reports or blogs of a dogfight seen overhead, Jermaine was looking for social media that mentioned the Maharaja while he was in America. He didn't have his own Facebook page or Instagram account or anything else but he appeared on those of others, his time in America spent much like any other teenage boy but with significantly more money and a host of security guards following him around.

We were all thoroughly absorbed by what we were doing, which is why we were so easy to catch by surprise. The only warning we got was the sound of the lock clicking open, the noise almost inaudible over our conversation, but Anna heard it and her head coming up made me look toward the lobby in time to see the front door fly open.

Palace guards in their floaty pants, tunics, and turbans stormed into the room. Each of them was armed with a deadly looking black assault rifle and they were all pointing at us. Involuntarily, I closed my eyes, the brain telling me I didn't want to see the volley of bullets that would cut me and my friends to pieces.

It never came though, no one fired a shot and when I cautiously reopened one eye and then the other, I saw the Maharaja's uncle walking toward me through a corridor of armed guards.

He looked directly at me, then said over his shoulder, 'Captain, tell your men they can lower their weapons. Lord Postlewaite, what are you doing here?' he asked the British dignitary, clearly baffled by his presence in my odd group. 'No, nevermind, I have a pretty good idea. Mrs Fisher, I must express how happy I am to see you alive.' Now I was confused. I hadn't voiced it because I didn't want to skew anyone's thoughts including my own, but the creepy and unpleasant uncle was my number one most likely suspect to be behind whatever is going on. He stepped closer and offered me his hand. I took it because I couldn't think of anything else to do.

The armed guards were all now looking relaxed, their weapons held loosely in one hand or slung to their backs which convinced me there was no intention to shoot us all. So, I asked the obvious question. 'What is going on?'

'That is a good question, Mrs Fisher. I must say that you gave me quite the scare just now. I hoped to catch you in your stateroom but you were not there and there was not only the sign of a scuffle, but the secret escape passage was lying open. I thought I was too late, and then when we checked the other rooms, we found them all to be empty as well. I am thankful that you are astute enough to seek shelter as a group, it has undoubtedly deflected any further attacks this evening.'

'Okay. That really didn't answer my question though.' I was way beyond being polite.

He pursed his lips, letting my impertinence slide, but then swished his gown to check where the couch was and took a seat on it. I sat too, taking a pew opposite him but sitting upright instead of relaxing so that my head was above his and I could look down at him. 'We haven't yet been properly introduced, Mrs Fisher. I am Zebrahim Azir Zebradim, younger brother to the Maharaja that was and uncle to the Maharaja that will be. It is my sacred duty to ensure the rightful Maharaja is crowned tomorrow and I believe there is a plot to overthrow the crown.' I performed a mental fist pump: I had it right again. Go Patricia. 'I believe General Aziz had planned a coup and may intend to assassinate the Maharaja at his coronation as a demonstration of power.'

His information wasn't adding up. 'Your Highness, if the general is planning a coup, why was it a royal guard that attacked me this evening?'

'Was it a guard, Mrs Fisher? Or just a man dressed as a guard?' He didn't wait for me to answer, the question was rhetorical. 'Of course, it might have been a royal guard. I have reason to believe the general has infiltrated the palace security at many levels and has men loyal to him everywhere. Can I ask how you were able to overcome the attack and survive?'

'Luck mostly, Your Highness. Lord Postlewaite inadvertently distracted him and I got in a lucky blow with a candlestick.'

'That's what happened,' chipped in Lord Edgar happily as if he had done something worthwhile.

'Ah, yes. I saw the candlestick on the floor along with feathers from a torn cushion.'

I decided to push my luck. 'My valet, Aladdin, claimed that the Maharaja I met today isn't the real Maharaja and now he is being held in a cell in a dungeon below this palace. Aladdin has been badly beaten, which he claims was at the hands of the royal guard.'

The Maharaja's uncle nodded as he listened, then flicked his eyebrows and smiled. 'You are not wrong, Mrs Fisher. My brother was so impressed when the sapphire was returned to us. He said the woman behind it must be quite brilliant and I can see that he was right. With my worry that the general may be planning a coup, I have put several unfortunate but necessary precautionary measures in place. One of them was to hire a double. My nephew is currently keeping a low profile. He will appear at the coronation because it has to be him and not the double that is crowned as the new Maharaja but until I can reveal who is behind the plan to overthrow the crown, I must keep him safe. It will be stressful enough exposing him to potential snipers for his coronation despite all the precautions we are taking. As for your valet; he threatened to expose the double as a fake, he wouldn't listen to reason and became violent. His injuries are unfortunate and the guard that assaulted him will be charged. Aladdin is being held on my orders though, I cannot have him disclosing our subterfuge when it would put the real Maharaja in direct danger. I will ensure a doctor is sent to treat his wounds and make him comfortable though.' Everything Prince Zebrahim claimed made perfect sense and sounded completely reasonable. It explained the presence of the double and Aladdin's incarceration. The prince even looked truly remorseful that Aladdin had been hurt.

'This doesn't explain the snake in my room or the man that tried to kill me with a sword a short while ago. Or the attack on our aircraft for that matter. And what about my friends?' I asked when I got that far down my mental check list. 'I will swear on the Holy Bible that they would not have

102

gone to the docks looking for alcohol instead of attending the banquet. They must have stumbled across something the conspirators were doing.'

Calmly, Prince Zebrahim replied, 'There is no evidence of that. If they interrupted the general's men doing something, I think it more likely they would be dead. Why go to the trouble of arranging for them to be discredited as drunkards?' He had an answer for everything. Which was annoying because I had no answers at all. 'At this time, I do not know why the aircraft was shot at or by who. That is a mystery we have people working on but one which we might never solve. As for the snake; I said earlier that it could just be a snake. They do get into the palace sometimes. The attack on you this evening though; that was quite deliberate. I cannot say who was behind it. Not yet anyway, but if the general has infiltrated the palace security as I suspect, he might be concerned about your snooping.' He paused to see if I had any questions. When I failed to ask one after a few seconds, he continued. 'So now you know the truth, Mrs Fisher. I hope you can accept my apologies for my deception and for the danger I unintentionally placed you in. If you wish to leave, I will arrange for a new private jet to take you to wherever in the world you may wish to go. If you choose to stay, I will ensure you meet the real Maharaja tomorrow at his coronation. I offer you my personal guarantee of safety and will leave a guard in every suite to further ensure your stay in Zangrabar suffers no further... complications. I only ask that you relax and allow us to be the hosts we intended to be.'

My friends all looked relieved to be out of the frying pan with no sign of a fire waiting for them. They also looked tired but then the day had been long and filled with excitement. I could see no way of arguing with the prince and his kind words. He wanted to reassure us and as next in line to the throne had taken his time to visit us in person. It was no small thing.

I bowed my head respectfully. 'Thank you, Your Highness. Your reassurances and explanation for the attack tonight are warmly received.' The visit appeared to be concluded but as he twitched to stand up, I had a final question. 'Why have you not moved against the general already if you believe he is planning a coup?'

The prince's mouth opened and then closed again. He paused for a second, then answered my question, 'Insufficient evidence.' Then he chuckled. 'I could use your help actually, Mrs Fisher. This was the little mystery my nephew alluded to in his telegram. When he wrote that, I was with him, and at the time we thought there might be something odd going on in the palace. It was my suggestion that he include it in his message just in case we wanted to get your opinion. The situation changed faster than I expected though, forcing the subterfuge with the double and everything that has happened recently.'

'I'm all ears,' I replied, ready to hear what he had to tell me.

He stood up though, straightening his robe and nodding to the captain of the guard. 'I would feel I was burdening you unfairly if I discussed it with you now, Mrs Fisher. I will be glad to meet with you tomorrow morning though. Please have your guard contact me when you are ready. It is already late, and your friends look tired.' To accentuate his point, I had to stifle a yawn. It was late and I needed some sleep, but I would have cast that aside to help if I could. Before I could cram the yawn back down and close my mouth, he backed away and gave a small bow. 'Goodnight, Mrs Fisher. Good night, Lord Postlewaite.' Then he glanced around the room at everyone else. 'I hope you all sleep well.' Then with a sweep of his robe, he departed, the guard filing out neatly behind him until there was no one left in Rick's room but my party.

We were all looking at one another and no one was saying anything until Hideki broke the silence. 'Soooo, I guess that's it for today then?' I

104

saw his eyes cut to Barbie; the two of them weren't planning any sleep soon.

I started toward the suite's door with Anna tucked under my arm and another yawn forcing my jaw open. Everyone followed. I was going to go to bed, and I hoped to sleep. There remained a stack of questions buzzing around my head; I wasn't at all satisfied about Aladdin being held in the dungeon, but I acknowledged that I couldn't do anything about it.

As I got outside, Jermaine caught up to me. 'Madam is there anything else I can do for you before I turn in? Would you feel safer if I slept in one of your suite's other bedrooms?'

I looped my arm through his and walked with him. 'You are too thoughtful, Jermaine.'

'It is my job, madam.'

'Not to this level of commitment, it isn't. I have all I need though and a personal guard to boot. I think you should get some sleep and see me in the morning.'

He leaned down to whisper. 'Madam, it would please me more to remain in your quarters tonight. I am... unsettled here.' Well that did it; I couldn't refuse him now that he wanted it for his own peace of mind.

'I could stay with you instead, Patricia,' piped up the ambassador, proving that hope springs eternal. This time all it took was a stern look for him to accept defeat. He bowed his head gracefully in my direction and walked away.

Looking back at it now, I'm shocked we lived through the night.

Coronation Day

I awoke just before six the next morning, logging less than five hours sleep but the sun was up and it was roughly my normal time to rise now that I visited the gym most days. Sitting in bed, I yawned and stretched and lazily considered pulling the covers over my head to go back to sleep. Exercise was keeping me young though, and while I hadn't thought about my naked body in years, now it was something I checked out in the mirror every day, critically assessing whether my face looked older, if my boobs were hanging lower.

Not that I thought going for a run was going to hold back the ravages of time forever. Giving them pause for thought was good enough reason though, so ten minutes after rising I was performing yoga on a mat in the living space.

The guard assigned to my suite was joined by Jermaine's when my butler collected his things to crash in the bedroom next to mine. The two guards must have rotated during the night as only one was visible now, standing near the lobby door looking bored but mostly alert.

I exercised in silence, the only sound that of my laboured breathing from the exertion. Thirty minutes of posing, holding, twisting and moving generated a light sheen of sweat and the need for a shower. By the time I came back out, the smell of coffee had filled the air of my suite. I was dressed for the morning in an expensive floral dress which I bought new in one of the Aurelia's high-end designer retail outlets especially for this trip.

Jermaine hadn't made it though. He was sitting in an armchair in the living area reading a newspaper. Just as he looked up, a valet, one of the ones from Rick or Akamu's suites came in bearing a tray on which tiny cups, a tall ornate coffee pot and other paraphernalia were balanced.

I gave him a smile of greeting. 'Good morning...'

'Fariq, Eminence,' he replied, placing the tray on a low table next to Jermaine. 'I have prepared fresh coffee; can I offer you some breakfast? We are able to cater to any taste.'

As he poured the dark brew into a cup for Jermaine, I joined him and asked for a cup myself. I had slept well but had woken filled with no less doubt than yesterday. Something was amiss and I worried that there were only a few hours to work out what it was.

I took the offered cup and thanked him, placing it under my nose to draw in a deep hit of the unctuous scent. He fell into a relaxed pose I recognised from watching Jermaine: he had no task until we gave him one so was waiting for instruction. I asked him a question. 'Fariq, you were looking after Mr Hutton originally, yes?'

'That is correct, Eminence.'

'You helped him with his ceremonial robes, I assume. Made sure he had them on correctly.'

'Yes, Eminence.'

'Were they well-tailored to him?'

'Yes, Eminence. A very good fit. Mr Hutton commented on it several times.'

'Did it strike you as odd that he chose to wear them to the docks?'

Fariq paused this time before answering, his smile drooping slightly. He recovered quickly though, smiling widely again as he thought of an answer. 'It is not my place to ask, Eminence.' It was an outright lie; his eyes had gone up and right to engage the creative part of his brain, not up and left to memory. This didn't really tell me anything I didn't already know but it proved there were lies being told. Fariq, unless he was someone important posing as a valet, was too low down the scale to be masterminding anything, so he was following orders from someone else. Were they the general's orders though? Or someone else's?

I didn't challenge him, instead I ordered breakfast, as did Jermaine – eggs with hummus and vegetables plus fruit juice. The coronation was to take place at two o'clock this afternoon on the steps of the palace in front of a huge crowd and television cameras from around the world. Between now and then, I needed to do minimal preparation because Osama Al-Kaisi had arranged for hairdressers and makeup artists. All I needed to do was sit and read a magazine while they buzzed around me and then get into the limousine that would take me to the red carpet – another influence from America the young Maharaja had embraced. All the official guests, including politicians, heads of state and a few pop stars, were to walk the red carpet where they could be photographed and interviewed. I wondered how that would sit with the Queen.

When Fariq returned ten minutes later to announce breakfast was served on the balcony, I asked him if there had been any message from Prince Zebrahim.

'No, Eminence,' he replied. 'No messages. Should I expect one?'

I didn't know the answer to that question. The prince had been quite clear that he intended to discuss with me General Aziz's movements but left it open regarding when that might happen today. Would he even have time? And if the general was planning a coup, was there any time to delay? Now that I thought about it, the prince's nonchalance over a potential military attack was crazy. Last night, in my sleep deprived state, it felt reasonable to leave it until this morning. Now, as I devoured my eggs and hummus, I found myself frowning in doubt.

109

Jermaine's phone chirped, an incoming text message attracting his attention. He leaned to look at the screen as he scraped together a piece of flatbread and hummus, then passed the device to me, pulling an expression that told me I needed to read it.

The message was from Barbie. She was with Deepa and they were on their way to the spa, was I ready? Baffled by the message, I dug around in my bag for my phone to discover that I had failed to charge it in all the pandemonium last night and it was quite dead. Barbie had most likely been texting or calling and getting no answer so had tried Jermaine instead.

I gratefully accepted Jermaine's phone and called her back. 'Barbie, hi, it's Patricia.'

'Hey, Patty. Did you lose your phone or forget to charge it?'

'The latter. What's this about a spa?'

I could tell from her voice that she was excited at the prospect of visiting another spa for free. Then I remembered Hideki and wondered if perhaps he might be the cause of her buoyant mood this morning. 'A servant arrived with a note on a silver tray this morning. Deepa got one as well. We are both invited to luxuriate ourselves in the palace spa this morning. I'm thinking deep tissue massage, reiki head massage, facial seaweed wrap, the full works. How about you?'

'I didn't get an invite,' I replied, my tone trying to decide between curiosity about why and disappointment that I didn't.

Barbie said, 'Oh,' sounding surprised, then, 'I'm sure it was just an oversight. The Maharaja refers to you as a national treasure. You should just come with us anyway.'

I almost said no, but why shouldn't I go? There was nothing else for me to do here except read a book and laze about. I could do most of that while a strong-fingered masseuse worked the worry from my shoulders. 'When are you going?'

'As soon as you are ready. My valet, Akim, is waiting to escort us there so we don't get lost. I still can't believe how big this place is.'

I took the phone away from my ear to check the time. 'I need five minutes.'

'Yay!' squealed my size-zero friend. 'I'll be at your door in two.' Then she was gone, undoubtedly grabbing her things and knocking for Deepa on her way to me.

'The palace has a spa,' I announced to my breakfast companion.

Jermaine had gone back to reading his paper, a copy of the New York Times, but looked over the top of it now. 'Nothing about that surprises me, madam. You are going with Barbie?'

'And Deepa. Will you mind Anna for me?'

He dipped his head. 'Of course, madam.'

I mopped up the last of the hummus with a piece of flatbread, downed my fruit juice and, with a light kiss to the top of his head, I left Jermaine on the balcony of my stateroom and went to get ready. My head, like Barbie's, was now filled with thoughts about what treatments would be available and how many hours we could stay in there until we would absolutely have to leave to attend the coronation ceremony.

A pang of guilt stabbed through me that Rick and Akamu were still incarcerated. I wanted to do something about it, I just couldn't work out what that ought to be. Typically for me, I was trying to find a way to

111

blame myself for their predicament even though I knew that made no sense. Maybe something would come to me while I was lying face down in the spa.

Well, it did, but not in the way I expected.

Invitation

Deepa, Barbie, and I were giggling like schoolgirls on our way to the spa as we trailed behind Akim. He said it wasn't far to go which it wasn't if you were using international travel as a yardstick. It took fifteen minutes to walk there but that gave Deepa and I a chance to press Barbie for details about her night with Hideki.

Deepa started it of course; it was not a subject I would ever raise, but when Barbie turned crimson and then started jabbering, I took my turn at teasing her. My observation that she liked him when I saw them kiss back in Japan had been right on the money. With her looks, Barbie could choose almost any man she wanted, but rarely did; it took someone special to get her attention.

'Will you stay in touch with him when he goes back to Tokyo?' Deepa asked.

Barbie nodded vigorously but I noted her expression was now tinged with sadness. 'I will. I don't see how it will work though. I don't mind some separation, but we won't see each other more than a couple of times a year. He is about to get his first-year residency assignment and is so excited to put all his training into practice.'

'Where is he going?' I asked.

'He doesn't know yet. He applied to several hospitals in America plus a few others in England and Australia and other English-speaking countries and to some in Japan just in case. He wants to travel, which I totally get, it was why I took the job with Purple Star Cruise Lines, but wherever he goes, it won't be where I am.'

I felt a little sorry for her, I faced a similar conundrum; what Alistair and I were going to do when the ship returned to Southampton in a few weeks. The countdown had already started, and I felt it booming in my ear when I gave it any thought. We hadn't really talked about it, only in the briefest terms but I still planned to get off the ship and his entire life was onboard it. I said none of that of course, it was Barbie's turn to talk about her concerns.

We continued chatting all the way there, finally arriving at the spa to find it filled with other ladies. It was a busy place. It was also even more luxurious and opulent than the rest of the palace. It was incredible. Carefully balanced lighting, pools of water and soft furnishings intertwined with yet more marble and gold made it the most enticing spa I had ever visited. It felt amazing just to be standing in it.

Akim left us at the door when a short woman of about my age met us. 'Please come inside ladies and welcome. Please follow me. I have strict instruction to treat you each as I might a goddess.' The woman led us to a changing room. 'You will find robes, towels and footwear in the private rooms beyond each of these doors. Refreshments are available so should you want anything you need only ask the servant attending you. I will leave you to undress and will be waiting for you outside. Please take your time.'

Once she departed, I breathed in deeply, holding the succulent and heady scents of the spa. This was going to be good.

And good it was. The spa was staffed only by women which made us feel more relaxed and comfortable about being naked beneath our robes. An hour passed as I reached a state of relaxation rarely achieved in my life. As I switched from having the knots worked from my muscles to having the tension eased out of my skull, a niggling thought surfaced: The vizier's staff was carved to form a cobra at the top. I remembered seeing it now. How had I forgotten that? Once that thought hit me, I started thinking about Mustafa. His uniform hadn't fitted him very well, but every single one of the royal guard I had seen so far was broad and muscular. Mustafa hadn't been either. Now that I thought about it, he reminded me of the clerics I saw following the vizier around. I had my eyes closed but inside my head I was squinting as I tried to connect more dots.

Who stands to gain? Perhaps this time my question needed to be, who stands to lose. If the new Maharaja intended to introduce sweeping reforms that would change the shape of his country, wouldn't he have to upset a lot of people to do so? He would unsettle or ruin powerbases where men had dominated for the nation's entire history. The vizier, as head of their religion, would be right at the top of that list with much to lose. Had he tried to kill me to prevent me from digging about? I had asked him about the Maharaja's mystery and less than two hours later I had a cobra in my room. Was that coincidence? I didn't think so.

What about the fighter plane that tried to shoot us down though? Was that his first attempt and did he have the connections to arrange it? That thought caused the general's face to flash in my mind. He must have the influence or ability to arrange a fighter aircraft. What would he lose or gain if the real Maharaja came to power and was able to introduce sweeping reforms? I didn't know the answer to that question, but the prince had all but accused him of treason.

Like a circle, my thoughts had ended up back on Prince Zebrahim. If the prince suspected the general was behind a plot to overthrow the crown then surely he should have moved against him already, sufficient evidence or not and where was the real Maharaja? The prince assured me last night that he was keeping a low profile until the coronation where he would reappear and then rule. Why wouldn't the Maharaja be safe at the banquet last night though?

My rambling thoughts were interrupted by a voice. A man's voice. Or rather the voice of a teenage boy. 'Ah, ladies, I see you received my invitation. I hope you are all feeling relaxed.'

The three of us had chosen to remain together for our treatment, the spa offering family sized rooms where groups could be treated simultaneously. However, neither Barbie, nor Deepa, nor I had anything on and now the fake Maharaja was staring at our naked bodies. The masseuses all hurried from the room without a word, leaving the three of us behind.

'Get out!' yelled Deepa, covering herself with a towel. Her shout echoed what Barbie and I were thinking and we reinforced the idea with our own voices.

He didn't move though, calmly raising a hand to beg us for quiet. 'I am the Maharaja, ladies. I have my own personal harem and have slept with over one thousand of this nation's most beautiful women.' The young fake king was flanked on either side by royal guards, they at least had the decency to cast their eyes downward.

Barbie wasn't to be cowed though. 'That's lovely, Your Majesty,' she said as she wrapped a towel around herself and sat back down on her massage table. 'Really, nice to know. What do you want?'

'I would have thought it obvious, babe. I want to make you rich. I want to lavish you with jewels and cars and set you up for the rest of your lives.'

'Why?' asked Deepa, suspicion all over her features.

The fake Maharaja raised his eyebrows as if surprised by her question. 'It is standard for all the women in my harem.'

'Your harem!' blurted Deepa and Barbie together.

'Yes. It is a great honour to join a Maharaja's harem and the rewards go far beyond the opportunity to bear my offspring. Offspring of a royal line.' I wanted to call him out now that I knew he wasn't the real Maharaja, but I wasn't on safe ground and provoking him might have repercussions on Rick and Akamu. He said he wouldn't interfere with law in Zangrabar but I'm sure he could call in a favour to make their stay here even less pleasant.

Instead, I said, 'I think I'm a little old to be producing offspring.'

He swung his gaze to look at me, noticing me for the first time perhaps as he gave a quick once over. 'Um, no I meant the other two, babe. I mean, you're okay in a MILF kind of way, but still a little old for me. Thanks for the offer and all but I'll stick with Miss Perfect Rack and her friend here.'

Barbie growled. 'Who taught you to speak to women like this, Your Majesty? You ought to be ashamed of yourself. We are not for sale. WE will not be joining your harem. And you can keep your money and jewels.' My blonde friend's chest was heaving with the adrenalin coursing through her, the fake Maharaja watching her breasts heave up and down each time she drew a breath. Noticing the grin on his face, she squinted at him, but then realised Deepa hadn't agreed with her statement. 'That's right, isn't it, Deepa?'

'Oh, err, yes. Yes, of course,' Deepa responded, snapping out of a personal dream that might have involved her own yacht and a Ferrari. 'Absolutely not,' she added to make her decision sound more firm. 'No joining of harems.'

The fake Maharaja seemed amused by us. 'Very well, ladies. If you change your minds...'

Then he turned about and led the two guards from the room. We were alone in the spa again, but I no longer felt like being here. I was incensed now, and it felt like high time I pulled the rug out from under the fake Maharaja's feet. Across from me, Barbie was gritting her teeth and frowning, muttering under her breath and possibly castrating the young king in her imagination.

'Barbie,' I called to get her attention. 'How would you like to help me poke around a little? I think the prince was lying last night when he said the real Maharaja is on board with everything that is happening. I think that if someone doesn't work out who is behind it all, that little twerp is going to be crowned and then become a puppet king for others to control.'

Then I told them what Aladdin had said about the real Maharaja's thoughts on women's rights and other long overdue reforms and about what I had pieced together so far.

'What do we need to do?' asked Deepa as she slid off the massage table.

'We get dressed,' I replied, heading to the door back to our private changing rooms. 'Then we get undressed again.'

Behind me both girls said, 'Huh?'

'I'll explain on the way.'

The Pilot

Akim wasn't waiting for us when we left the spa as we imagined he might be, so we tried to find our own way back to the wing that housed our staterooms. The problem was that the palace was not only enormous and vast but was symmetrical, so one piece looked like the mirror image of another piece. Or, to put it another way, everything looked the same. Ten minutes into our return trip, I had to admit we were lost.

'I think we took a wrong turn back at the fountain,' said Deepa.

Barbie pulled a face. 'Which one?'

Deepa shrugged.

'I'm just going to ask someone, okay?' I wasn't inclined to walk around the palace for the next hour looking for our rooms and our mission was time sensitive.

'Can I help you ladies?' The voice came from across the hall as a man emerged from a room. He wore Zangrabarian garb, which is to say he had on a tunic and loose-fitting pants plus a turban. He looked dressed to attend the coronation in a few hours. He also looked familiar.

'Thank you,' I replied automatically. 'That is very generous of you. We have become a little disorientated.'

He asked, 'Where is it you are trying to get to, Mrs Fisher?'

I looked at his face again. He knew my name and addressed me as if he knew me. 'I'm sorry, have we met?'

The man smiled more deeply this time, taking in Barbie and Deepa as well as he said, 'I was your pilot for the journey here. Once again let me apologise for the discomfort endured.'

'Goodness,' said Barbie. 'It is we who should be thanking you. You got us here alive and unharmed. Were it not for your skill, I dread to think what might have become of us.'

The pilot inclined his head to accept the praise. 'Now how may I assist you, ladies?'

I could see that Barbie was about to tell him where we were trying to get to but a question had occurred to me. 'Do you know what type of aircraft attacked us? Have they identified what nation it was from?'

'They?' he asked, baffled by the question.

'Yes, surely there is an enquiry underway to determine the source of the threat?'

'Not that I am aware of, Mrs Fisher. No one has spoken to me about the incident.'

'Sorry,' I replied. 'My mistake.' Now my mind was whirling. The prince had flat out lied to me about it. I barely registered Barbie asking the pilot to direct us back to our staterooms but when he elected to escort us there, my feet shuffled along after them on their own accord.

The prince had lied about the investigation. Not that it came as that much of a shock because I felt fairly certain he was lying about other things as well, like the real Maharaja knowing what was going on for one. What did it mean though? If he wasn't bothering to instigate an enquiry into shots being fired at one of the Maharaja's personal jets, then it had to be because he already knew who was behind it. That startling revelation hurried my pace, quickly catching up with the girls and the pilot to urge them on.

As we arrived gratefully back in the passageway containing our staterooms, I thanked the pilot and shook his hand. There was no time to waste now though; we needed to check something and ask some questions and then it was going to be time to solve this case. I wasn't sure we would make it out of the country alive if we didn't.

Deepa, Barbie, and I each knocked on one of the boys' doors, waiting in the passageway for them to appear. Then with Jermaine, Martin and Hideki in tow, we went to my place to map out what had to happen next.

Ten minutes later, Hideki said, 'That's insane.'

Barbie laughed at him. 'You think that's mad? You should have been there when we all dressed up as zombies.' He screwed his face up in disbelief. 'This will work out fine, babe,' she said and kissed his cheek.

Martin took out his sidearm, I hadn't known he was carrying it, but it had been tucked into the waistband of his trousers. 'No time to waste then,' he said as he checked the chamber and looked along the top to make sure the sights were aligned. 'We'll see what we can see and meet you there, yes?'

Deepa said, 'Be careful,' and Barbie kissed Hideki on the lips then the three men departed, Jermaine taking Anna with him as a flimsy pretence that the chaps were just out for a walk. The departure left us girls looking at each other.

'We're really going to do this?' asked Barbie.

I shrugged, but Deepa said, 'Yeah. Let's go be prostitutes. It'll be fun.'

I was known for dreaming up daft plans and this was definitely one of them. It came down to a question about men and how predictable they were. Listening to the fake Maharaja boast about all the women he had slept with made me think about the poor girls in the harem. Maybe I shouldn't pity them, maybe they were there voluntarily and well rewarded. I didn't know but I wouldn't change places with them no matter what was on offer.

The thought that occurred to me though, was how pliable Charlie had always been after sex. He would open up and talk about things. At least, he did on the occasions that he didn't fall straight to sleep and then I really only meant in the early stages of our marriage when having sex was new and exciting. On the way back from the spa, just before we got lost and met the pilot, I asked Deepa and Barbie about it. They both agreed; men are rubbish. At precisely the point when they have rolled over onto their backs, they will grant you any wish, agree to any deal, and talk about whatever you want to talk about.

I was willing to bet the same thing happened in the harem so the secrets those girls must know... well, I had a few very pointed questions to ask and that was where we were going right now. We had to get directions, choosing one of the laundry ladies to ask rather than a man who would almost certainly claim to have no idea.

The woman eyed us suspiciously, but told us how to find it, ending her directions by saying, 'And then follow your nose. They're behind the door that smells like whores.' It was clear she disapproved of them and of our interest in them, probably assuming that Barbie and Deepa were here to sign up and I was... well, I don't know what assumption she might have made about me, but we had directions and found it first time.

It actually smelled like soap and expensive perfume rather than whatever a person might imagine a gathering of whores might smell like. The door was locked so Barbie knocked.

A small panel at eye height slid back to reveal a set of eyes behind it. They were a woman's eyes but not a young woman. It was all I could see of her, though I heard her voice when she demanded, 'What do you want?'

'We came to join up?' said Barbie as if we were enlisting into the Army. 'The Maharaja invited us in person this morning.'

It seemed we were expected because the hatch slid shut again and the door opened inwards, then closed again as soon as we were inside. The woman on the other side of the hatch was in her seventies and had the air of someone who was used to being in charge. She looked each of us up and down, nodding at Barbie and prodding her chest. Barbie held her breath and put up with it. Then she moved onto Deepa and did the same thing. 'Yes, I'm not surprised. He has been complaining about repetition. You're a surprise though.' Her final comment was aimed at me.

I thought about giving her a snappy comeback, but I needed to get into the harem and not get thrown out, so I smiled instead. 'Men have such eclectic tastes, don't they?'

She didn't look like she knew what eclectic meant but she turned and led us away from the door. 'This way, ladies. You'll need to get changed. If he knows there are new girls in here, it won't be long before he arrives, even on his coronation day and there will be lots of other men through here over the next few days while he hosts everyone. It should calm down a little after that but remember; you are here to please, not be pleased. You do what they ask you to: two, three or twelve at a time.'

I shuddered at the thought, but we had arrived in a central lounge area where more than two dozen girls were lounging around reading magazines or books and doing very little. Each of them was wearing the same outfit in one of a variety of colours. Hues of pastel, pinks, blues, greens and more in tiny panties and a camisole top. Most also wore stockings though it seemed a personal choice whether they selected hold ups, a suspender belt or something else. Everyone one of the girls looked to be Zangrabarian and each of them had been chosen for her looks.

A girl with blonde and pink highlights in her black hair said, 'Oh, thank goodness. Reinforcements.' She unfolded from a chair, waving at the older lady. 'It's okay, Bethansa, I'll take it from here.' Oddly I had expected jealousy among the established toward the new recruits, but they all seemed genuinely pleased to see us.

As Bethansa departed, Pink Highlights invited us to sit. 'Hi, I'm Irina. I'll introduce you to everyone later but there's a few of us so don't be ashamed when you can't remember all the names.'

'How many of you are there?' asked Deepa

'Almost one hundred. You'd think that meant we got time off between visits but this place is popular and the Maharaja likes to share it with visiting dignitaries and anyone he feels like rewarding. The old Maharaja that is, not the new one. We don't really know about the new one.'

'How come?' I asked, making her attention swing to me. 'I was given to understand that he is a regular here.'

'He is,' she conceded. 'But only for the last week. None of us ever saw him before that.' If I didn't already know that the Maharaja I met was the fake, then this would have been evidence enough to convince me.

'Would you like a drink of something?' Irina asked. 'Not that we have alcohol if that is what you intend to ask. Mellua can make a mean sweet apple tea though. You should take on plenty of water too, you'll want to stay hydrated.'

'Why is that?' asked Barbie while looking very unsure that she wanted to hear the answer.

'Let's just say that new girls are always the most popular. I remember my first day here so take my word for it that you need to watch out for chafing.' All three of us crossed our legs simultaneously.

We had broken the ice, the bit which I thought was going to take the most effort. Now it was time to ask some questions. 'Does Prince Zebrahim visit often?'

Irina smiled at me. 'So that's why you are here. He is a handsome man, isn't he?'

I played along. 'I hoped you might be able to tell me what his policies are on reform of the country and how he felt about his brother's rule.'

Silence ruled for several heartbeats as all the girls in their underwear stared at the three of us still fully clothed and for a moment, I thought they were going scream for help. Irina was no dummy though, 'You're not here to join the harem at all, are you?'

There was no choice now but to reveal the truth. I pursed my lips shook my head. Then I told them the truth. With Deepa and Barbie backing me up, I convinced them that the young Maharaja who had been visiting them so recently was a fake and that the real Maharaja was most likely being held captive somewhere. I explained about his plans to transform Zangrabar, at which point one girl had gushed that they might now get Starbucks and MTV. They got it though and they got why this would be a good thing for the country and the generations of women to follow them.

Then they told us everything they knew: All the little secrets men bragged about in bed, the secret connections between men that no one outside knew about, and the deals that were brokered inside the harem that the men involved believed the girls were too dumb to understand.

I had it all. Now I had to work out what to do with it because there still wasn't anyone in the palace I could take this to. Just as I was pondering what my next move was, Bethansa wandered back into the room. She had someone with her. 'Your usual today, sir? Or would you like to wait for the twins?'

I glanced around as my eyes caught the movement and had to do a double take when I saw who it was. 'Lord Edgar,' I said in greeting as calmly and politely as I could. His face turned deep beetroot. Because I felt like being cruel, I indicated around the room with one hand. 'Which one of these lucky ladies is your, um... usual?' I smiled sweetly at him.

Across the room, a small woman in light blue underwear slowly raised her hand like a schoolchild who thought she might know the answer but wasn't sure if it had been a trick question.

'I, um,' he stuttered.

I stood up. 'Nevermind, we're leaving. You have lots of fun now.'

Then a hammering from outside got everyone's attention. The look of surprise on Bethansa's face told me something unusual was happening but Jermaine's shout told me what it was before anyone could move. 'Madam? Madam are you in there?'

Barbie had raced to the door, yanking it open to let the three men spill in. They were all out of breath, looking to have run hard to reach us. 'We don't have much time, madam. They are right behind us.'

'Who,' asked Barbie. 'Who's behind you?'

He sucked in a lungful of air and tried to get his breathing under control. 'The vizier's clerics and some of the royal guard. More were joining the chase as we fled. You were right though.'

'Yeah,' said Martin Baker. 'You were very right. He saw us looking at him though, knew we had identified him, and all hell broke loose. Hideki fought a couple of them off as we escaped the temple but there were too many. I didn't dare draw my weapon but what do we do now? They are on to us and we are trapped.'

'What?' asked Irina. 'What is going on?'

I grabbed her shoulders. 'Irina, we need your help. We are going to find the real Maharaja and rescue him, but if the guards catch us and detain us the fake Maharaja will get crowned today and the country will be ruled by Prince Zebrahim and those loyal to him.'

'What do you need us to do?'

'Is there a back way out of here?'

'Several,' she said, her colleagues crowding around us as they all took an interest in helping.

Then more hammering echoed through from the door. Jermaine locked eyes with me, his expression apologetic. 'Oh, cripes, they found us already. I thought we had more time, madam. You go and we will hold them off.' Having made his heroic statement, he turned to face the door and twisted his neck one way and then the other to free it off, then rolled his shoulders. Hideki did likewise, preparing himself to delay the hoard so we could escape and maybe save the Maharaja.

That was when I noticed the incongruity. 'Where's Anna?' I asked, checking the floor but knowing already that she wasn't here.

Jermaine's head drooped as he faced me once more. 'She evaded me, madam. As we ran away, her lead slipped from my grasp and she ran back towards the guards and clerics that were chasing us. I should have gone after her.'

I shook my head. 'You would not have caught her. She is too fast and turns on a penny. You ought not to blame yourself and should not worry too much about her. She lived with gangsters and had bitten several murderers in the last few weeks. Chances are she is off finding the Maharaja before we can.' I was making a joke of it but I genuinely wasn't that worried about her because I had a pretty good idea where she was going.

Then someone outside hammered on the door again. This time they shouted as well. 'You come out here right now, Edgar Postlewaite. I know you're in there. Come out and face me.'

I looked at the ambassador. 'Oh, bugger,' he sighed, the colour draining from his face.

'Um, who is that?' I enquired, suspecting that I could guess the answer well enough for myself.

'My wife,' he admitted quietly. 'Take me with you,' he begged, falling to his knees to beg for mercy. 'I beseech you, don't let her find me here again.'

'Again?' I was sorely tempted to just open the door and let her in, not least because of my own experience with a cheating husband. I didn't though just in case she had fifty soldiers standing silently behind her and because Lord Edgar might yet prove useful. No. He was coming with me and we were all getting out of here. Once again, I locked eyes with Irina, who seemed to be the harem spokesperson. 'When did you ladies last take an excursion?'

Escape

There wasn't a lot of time if Jermaine was to be believed so while Lady Postlewaite hammered at the harem's door, I devised a plan to get us out without being caught. The biggest issue was that we were easy to spot. Jermaine was tall and black, Barbie was tanned but her blonde hair gave her away and none of us were dressed like the locals. If we had been in a kitchen, I would have opted to put on the uniform of the kitchen staff, but we were in a brothel, so we were going to have to wear lingerie.

Again.

This time though, it wasn't just me dressing up, it was everyone. The harem ladies had some trouble finding anything that would fit Jermaine though Martin and Hideki were more reasonably proportioned. Lord Edgar threw off his clothes with enthusiasm, seeming only too happy to put on ladies' underwear.

Wigs were added along with makeup and we hid Jermaine as best we could among the crowd by having him scooch down. The seven of us were dressed like all the other girls in the harem though, each wearing a different shade of camisole and panties. I could see the chaps' hairy chests beneath their see-through tops, there was nothing better we could do at short notice though. I just hoped no one looked too closely.

The chaps were not entirely happy about it, but they didn't argue either and just as we heard the rumble of many feet on the floor outside, Bethansa led us to a back door. With a grim smile, since she knew she was the one left to explain where all the concubines had gone, Bethansa shut the door with her left inside.

The rest of us had escaped.

Where had we escaped to though? Better yet, where were we safe to go to now? If the vizier's clerics and the royal guards were chasing us, then we couldn't go back to our staterooms to change or regroup. We were together but we had no direction.

Our singular task now was to find the real Maharaja and with him at our side, reveal the plot to steal his throne away. I didn't know where he was though. Right now it was a secondary concern, the first task was to evade capture from the guards who surely wouldn't take long to work out where we had gone.

The back door exited to stairs that led down to the gardens on the lee side of the building away from the coronation ceremony set up just beyond the palace wall on the other side. I guessed the door was so that husbands such as Lord Edgar could escape when someone came for them, but we were a gaggle of ladies in their lingerie and would attract attention as soon as we were spotted.

Led by Irina and closely followed by the rest of us with the chaps sandwiched in the middle where they were harder to see, we snaked along the wall of the palace with the ornate gardens to our left.

A shout rang out from the top of the stairs which made most of the girls jump in fright and several of them squeal. The pursuing pack had spotted us before we could reach a corner and slip away and now it was a foot race.

'Go,' insisted Irina with a shove to my shoulder and I heard her say, 'Good luck,' as Barbie grabbed my hand and we started running. Deepa and the others easily kept pace with me, but Lord Edgar was in no shape to be running anywhere, or visiting a harem for that matter so Jermaine was dragging him along by his camisole. Ahead of us was a corner of the palace and most likely an entrance to be found just around it. If we could slip back inside, perhaps we could find more suitable clothing and find our way back to the dungeons to look for the Maharaja.

Barbie breached the corner a foot or so ahead of me and grabbed the wall to swing herself around it. 'In here,' she yelled as she pelted through a door. It looked like a maintenance area or boiler room if the steel door was anything to go by, and it had a double width roller door next to it with a road leading in.

As we burst from the light into the dark, my vision couldn't adjust quickly enough so I didn't see that Barbie had slammed on her brakes and almost tumbled over in her attempt to curtail her forward motion. I slammed into her which created a pile up as Martin, then Deepa, then Hideki all fell over us. Only Jermaine remained on his feet. From my position on the dirty floor, I had to wonder why he was alone and where Lord Edgar could have gone. Not that it would make any difference; the vast room we had inadvertently run into contained hundreds of palace guards and dozens of heavily armed looking vehicles. This was the precaution the prince had spoken of. If the general planned a coup, the prince had forces poised to repel it. Our visit to the harem had told me why the general was going to attack and why. I had almost run out of questions to ask and felt that I possessed almost all the answers.

Suddenly though, the only question I had was whether they would execute us by beheading or a different method.

Surprise Visitors

The cells were all arranged along one wall so none of us could see anyone else. We could talk even though there wasn't much to say, but without mirrors, we could only see the inside of our own cells and the wall opposite.

Deepa was in the cell next to mine, but I was at the end of the line so had no one to the other side and hadn't seen who went into the cell on the other side of hers. The silence after they shut the doors stretched on for a little while, but Martin Baker found his voice first, speaking loudly so that everyone could hear. 'I think they all left. Is everyone alright?'

He got back a chorus of despondent positive replies. Everyone was uninjured but we were incarcerated and, though no one said it, I felt sure they planned to kill us. How could they let us go? I spent all that time trying to work out who I could trust when the answer was nobody. The vizier, Prince Zebrahim, the general; they were all playing a part in this conspiracy.

The fake Maharaja was going to be assassinated by the general but the general was being tricked by the prince who intended to remove his nephew and emerge as the hero after he fought the general and his men. The general would be conveniently killed in the exchange of bullets so he couldn't reveal the conspiracy.

I think each of us explored our cells, I could hear the others grunting as they looked for a weak connection on the bars and scratching at the floor to see how far they descended into it. They were solid though, built centuries ago when contracts never went to the lowest bid. We were not going to get out this time and no one was coming to rescue us.

'Patty?' Barbie's voice echoed along the corridor.

'Yeah?'

'It's not your fault, you know?' I didn't say anything. 'I know how you like to blame yourself when things go wrong, but you couldn't know what we were walking into when you invited us to come with you on this trip.'

'We have escaped from worse than this, madam,' added Jermaine, doing his best to keep peoples' spirits up.

The coronation was in an hour though. Prince Zebrahim would enact his plan and become the new Maharaja with no one left to oppose him. How could anyone stop him now.

'Quiet, someone's coming,' hissed Martin, silencing the snippets of conversation passing back and forth along the cells.

I listened and sure enough, there were voices coming our way. They didn't sound right though, which is to say they didn't sound like Zangrabarian guards. Instead, they sounded Irish and it was women speaking. In a country where women were unable to hold any proper jobs unless they were domestic, menial or involved having sex, what would women be doing in the dungeon?

The answer was more surprising than I would have believed.

As my cell was the first one in line, I was the first one to see Rick's silly beaming face appear around the edge of my cell door. Then Akamu swung into view and he was quickly followed by Agnes and Mavis, the two expert thieves and con artists who helped me on the Aurelia when it was quarantined.

'I said we would find them in a dungeon,' said Akamu, Rick silently handing over a ten dollar note with a grumpy expression.

'Who's that?' asked Barbie. 'Is that Akamu?'

Then Rick spotted my outfit and his eyes popped out of his head. 'What are you wearing?

'Nevermind that, what are you doing here? How did you get out? Where did you come from, ladies?' My questions came as a torrent, buoyed to the surface by a big balloon of hope as Agnes swung a big ring of keys around her wrist.

'What's going on?' demanded Barbie, unable to see anything from her cell but her voice was joined by Martin, Deepa, and Hideki as they too tried to find out who I was talking to.

None of them spoke though, moving aside to let a fifth person approach. 'Hello, Patricia,' said the British ambassador, taking the keys from Agnes as he stepped up to my cell door. 'Perhaps now I will earn a way into your heart.' I saw that he tried really hard to keep his eyes looking at mine but ultimately, he failed, glancing down at my barely covered body and back up to find me staring at him, my cheeks glowing with embarrassment.

'If only it was my heart you were after, Lord Edgar,' I replied, pushing my luck even though he quite literally held the key to my escape. I had to acknowledge his achievement though; here were my friends and they were unharmed.

Shaking off my comment he explained, 'I tripped on a root and fell into a bush. When your butler looked back for me, I could see him, but I don't think he could see me. He hesitated, but ultimately, he had to chase after you. No one else could see me either, so I waited for them all to pass and snuck back to the harem to collect my clothes. On my way out of the palace, I spotted these two gentlemen and recognised them for what they were straight away.'

135

Rick and Akamu still wore their fancy banquet clothes with the gold pants. My head was filling with questions again, so I went with the one at the top of the list. 'How did you get away from the authorities?' I asked Agnes and Mavis.

Mavis tutted. 'What? You don't think those idiots could hold us, do you? We were out within a day.'

'We even went back in disguised as cleaners to let Max and Amy out,' boasted Agnes. 'We probably could have robbed the place too. They are so wrapped up in looking for criminals that they never think to look at the people around them. So, we came here looking for the boys. We have unfinished business, don't we?' she asked Rick. I watched as she slipped her hand into his and the two exchanged a glance.

Lord Edgar started trying keys in my door. Just like last night though, none of the keys opened the lock. Bored, Mavis shouldered the ambassador out of the way, pulling two pins from her hair as she bent down to look in the lock. 'Agi, give me a hand here.'

The two women fiddled with the lock for a few seconds, looking at the ceiling as they worked three long pins into the movement and using skills honed over decades, they turned the lock.

I was free!

Rick moved to Deepa's cell, calling out, 'We'll have you all out in a jiffy.' Then waved to Barbie in the next cell as the two Irish ladies started on the next lock.

I gave Lord Edgar a hug; he had come to rescue me after all, but when I tried to let go a second later, I found his arms were locked around my waist. He wasn't letting go and I had to poke him in the ribs when the hug went into the fifth second because it was getting weird.

136

'Do you want to hear what happened to us?' asked Akamu.

'You stumbled on the secret passage at the far end of your suite, saw the vizier heading along it with a snake in his hands and were grabbed by his clerics. They injected you with pure alcohol and dropped you off near the docks so the police would arrest you for public inebriation.'

'Yeah,' said Akamu, bafflement crossing his face. 'I still don't know how you do that.'

'It was the only explanation I could come up with. They didn't want to kill you before the banquet but were probably going to arrange for something to happen to you while you were in jail.'

'Sounds terrible,' Mavis commented, screwing up her face at the thought. 'Good thing we were able to track you down.'

'Hi, I'm Hideki,' said Hideki, joining us in the passageway as the last one to be freed.

Barbie gave him a hug, then asked, 'Don't we need to get going?'

I nodded. 'Now that we are all out, yes. We need to split up though.'

Barbie didn't follow. Neither did anyone else from the sea of confused faces around me. 'We have to find the real Maharaja. He is the one that will bring this to a stop. The guards and soldiers are doing as they are told because they think their orders come from the Maharaja; none of them know he is fake, only a few people do. One of them is Aladdin, the Maharaja's personal valet since birth. He is down here in the dungeons somewhere too. We have to find him as well. We also have to attend the coronation.

I grabbed Rick's arm and twisted it, 'Hey! Hurting!' he complained.

137

I needed to see the time on his watch. 'We have just enough time to get changed and get to the coronation.'

'Why on earth would we want to do that?' asked Barbie, utterly baffled by my suggestion.

For me it was obvious. 'There's a couple of bits I still haven't worked out. I think I have it all but if we turn up unexpectedly at the ceremony, the mastermind behind it all will have to deal with us. If we have the Maharaja, that is when we reveal him. It will stop everyone dead in their tracks, but the ringleader will try to find a way to finish their plan anyway. You lot need to get changed.'

'Changed into what?' asked Martin.

'Anything less conspicuous would be a start.' He looked down at his camisole and conceded the point.

As a group we migrated away from the cells and to a junction. 'We came this way,' said Lord Edgar, pointing down one corridor. 'It leads to a staircase that exits in the gardens.'

I glanced along the passageway, squinting into the distance down all four options until I saw what I hoped I would: a small mark on the wall. It was one of the direction marks Jermaine scratched in last night so we wouldn't get lost.

'Can you lead everyone back to the suites, Lord Edgar? They all need to get changed and attend the coronation.'

'I guess so,' he replied looking unsure. 'What will you do?'

'I'm going to take these two master lock pickers and the keys, and I am going to find the real Maharaja. Then I'm going to smuggle him into the coronation disguised as a valet.'

'I'm coming with you, madam,' insisted Jermaine, his tone making it clear there was no sense in arguing.

'Goodness, Patty,' sighed Barbie, 'this is all so risky again. Good luck.'

'There's no time to lose,' snapped Martin, getting the team moving with urgent gestures. 'Let's get this done and save the country.'

Oh, my life. He was right. What we did in the next hour went way beyond saving our own lives, it would impact the entire nation and very possibly global politics. The new Maharaja would guide Zangrabar and the region into a new era of understanding, women's rights and enlightenment. His uncle, the general and the vizier might cast it back into the dark ages.

We all reached the mark on the wall, Lord Edgar and most of the team going right, myself, Jermaine, Agnes, and Mavis going left. There were a few quick hugs and good lucks but then the four of us were alone and the plan relied on me being able to find the most important and powerful man in the country.

I found Aladdin still in his cell and still bloody and bruised, proof that Prince Zebrahim had lied about sending a doctor to treat him.

'What are you wearing?' he croaked through the bars at me as the ladies worked on the lock. I already knew the bunch of keys wouldn't open this lock so hadn't even tried. He was clearly very thirsty, his mouth so dry he could barely speak. I had no water with me, but Jermaine ran off to fetch some, returning less than a minute later, just as Agnes and Mavis popped the cell door open.

Aladdin had been left to rot with no food or water, a barbaric treatment regardless of the crime. It had been less than twenty-four hours thankfully and he wasn't weakened by his ordeal in any noticeable way. Once he sipped the water and got some moisture into his parched mouth, he said, 'I need to find the real Maharaja.'

'That is where we are going next,' I replied.

'Only we don't know where he is,' pointed out Jermaine.

Aladdin started moving, the rest of us following now we had a direction to go in. He talked as he hurried along, 'I have had all night to think about it. I doubt they put him in a dungeon. There would be too much chance of one of the guards finding him. I realised last night that everyone is loyal to the crown: the soldiers, the royal guards. I don't think they know the Maharaja has been replaced so they would need to hide him somewhere that he couldn't escape from and would never be accidentally discovered in.'

'So where is that?' asked Mavis.

Aladdin picked his pace up. 'The north tower.'

The north tower did exactly what it said on the tin: It was a tall round tower jutting up above the rest of the palace to give unparalleled views across the kingdom and it was at the northmost point of the main palace building. Unfortunately, Aladdin had no better idea of his way around the dungeons than any of the rest of us, so he rushed to a junction as if he knew where to go, then stopped and looked around while tapping his teeth in uncertainty.

Sensing the issue, I asked, 'Can you find your way there once we are back in the palace?'

'Yes, of course, I know the palace like the back of my ha...' I grabbed his arm and shoved him back in direction we came from last night as the series of small marks on the wall proved to be invaluable again. We had to get to the top of the spiral stairs, once again pushing myself to tackle the damned things in one go and once again having to wait for the older persons to catch up.

When we got to the passageway behind the suites, I saw the first open wooden panel and went through it, calling out as I brought the others in behind me. 'Cooee! It's Patricia. Are you decent?'

Akamu's rumbling voice echoed back from somewhere. 'In here. Did you find the Maharaja?'

'Not yet,' I said as I rounded the door to his bedroom. He was already mostly dressed in a fine suit but struggling to get the tie right.

'I never could stand wearing these things,' he complained. Mavis moved to help but failed to reach him because I snagged her arm. 'There'll be time later, I swear.'

Akamu was good enough to reinforce the need for action. 'I got this. Go be a hero, lady.' Then he gave her a peck on the lips and we were moving again, out of his stateroom's front entrance and left, following Aladdin on our way to the tower.

I had no idea what we would find, my imagination telling me it would be a bleak, open space with bare floorboards. The young king would be locked inside wearing loose rags and be half starved or dying of thirst. We had to get there yet, a task which proved difficult as we only got ten yards before three royal guardsman came around the corner ahead of us.

Both parties paused for a heartbeat, us realising we were trapped and there was no way they wouldn't realise who we were, and them taking a half second to look at the tall black man and the middle-aged woman dressed as Arabian whores and decide we were a problem to be dealt with.

Aladdin tried to reason with them. 'You have to listen to me. You all know who I am...'

'Yeah, you're the disgraced former valet to the Maharaja,' snapped the one in the middle, brandishing a sword. 'You were fired from that position and are involved in a plot to kill the Maharaja to get your revenge. Prince Zebrahim has ordered that you all be killed on sight.' The time for talking was over apparently as his colleagues also drew their swords and all three advanced on us.

Aladdin gibbered as he tried to work out something new to say. Nothing came and I was as lost for words as he. Jermaine pushed in front of me, looking to tackle three men with swords. It was a hopeless gesture though; we were trapped in a passageway with nowhere to go.

We could run though. I wanted to save the Maharaja, but I wasn't suicidal. Surviving to fight another day might allow me to return with better odds, or just put Zangrabar from my mind and never think of it again as long as I live. I grabbed Jermaine's arm. 'Fists can't beat swords.'

'Bullets can though,' growled Martin Baker stepping around me with his sidearm raised.

Deepa Bhukari went to the other side, her own weapon trained on the royal guardsmen. 'Drop the swords,' she ordered.

The guard that spoke previously did so again. This time with a smile on his face, 'I don't think so.' Then he gave the sword a swish and stepped forward, clearly meaning to attack her first.

Deepa shrugged and pulled her trigger.

With a squeal, the guard dropped his sword and fell to the ground. He called her some unrepeatable names as he clutched at his foot. She had shot off his pinky toe!

Deepa pointed her gun at the next guard in line. Both remaining guards raised their free hands in surrender and placed their swords on the floor.

'Oh, my goodness, what's happening?' asked Barbie, rushing into the passageway as everyone else also spilled from their rooms. The shot had drawn them all which was a good thing because my plan to turn up at the coronation just got a great deal harder with a death sentence hanging over us.

'Change of plan,' I announced. 'The prince has ordered that we all be killed on sight.'

'That's good of him,' growled Rick. 'You think we did something to upset him?'

Ignoring his glib question, I said, 'I think we ought to stay together now, splitting up just got exponentially more dangerous.'

Martin still had his gun pointing at the royal guards. 'What do we do with these three?'

'We have to tie them up.'

'I have some handcuffs,' volunteered Barbie. Then said, 'What?' as her cheeks coloured from my raised eyebrow.

As it turned out we didn't need Barbie's bedroom handcuffs. Deepa had packed her standard utility belt that went with her uniform and in that were some plasticuffs. Meeting the guards had delayed us another ten minutes, however with them secured inside Rick's suite, and Jermaine and I dressed in the two uniforms that didn't have blood on them, the entire group set off for the north tower once more. We got a little further this time.

With twelve of us in the group, sneaking about wasn't exactly easy, and the palace was filled with people scurrying here and there on various errands. Twice we had to duck down a corridor to avoid more of the royal guard and when we reached a wide atrium, we crossed it one at a time, like a military platoon, running quickly to cover the open space before regrouping on the other side.

The vastness of the palace meant it took fifteen minutes to reach the base of the tower which was accessed from the ground floor. Once inside the door at the bottom, I stopped everyone, a finger to my lips to keep them quiet. 'This place must have a guard on the door. We won't know if it is one or none or a battalion until we get up there though.' I saw Rick looking at the stairs with a weary look. 'Jermaine and I will go ahead. If there are guards up there, they will see our turbans first and think it is their replacements coming. Deepa and Martin should come with us as they are armed but everyone else should stay here and keep out of sight. This will get easier once we have the Maharaja.'

'I should come with you, Eminence,' suggested Aladdin. 'The Maharaja may be confused about who you are.' No one voiced any argument, so with the most basic of plans worked out, I waved him forward to lead the way and set off up the stairs.

Would there be a bit of this that finally went our way?

Don't be daft.

The North Tower

The tower was empty. I was wrong about it being a squalid and terrible place though; it was luxurious. The correct term for it a gilded cage if my memory served me correctly.

My nervousness which had started about eight hours ago now, reached a crescendo at the top of the stairs, but we found no one guarding the door. At that point, I berated myself for not bringing Agnes and Mavis to pick the lock, but the door wasn't locked. Initially, I assumed Aladdin had just got it wrong and dragged us from one end of the palace to the other, ducking guards and servants when the Maharaja was actually stashed somewhere else. That wasn't the case though; the tower was decked out in a manner suitable for a king and Aladdin seemed certain he had been here.

'This pot is still warm, madam.' Jermaine found a coffee pot, the contents of which had not yet cooled to room temperature, so we hadn't missed him by much.

'And these clothes are his size, Eminence,' added Aladdin.

From her position near the door, Deepa asked, 'What next? Where would they have taken him?' I walked over to the window and looked down. From up here we had an enviable view over the palace grounds and could see the coronation ceremony starting.

Then a thought struck me. 'How do you kill a head of state when they are always surrounded by bodyguards or travelling in a bullet proof car?' I asked the question of everyone in the room.

'Shoot their plane out of the sky?' suggested Martin.

Deepa said, 'Poison their food. Or hire a person prepared to give their life in exchange for the other person's. It's hard to defend against someone who is willing to die – a suicide bomber doesn't even need to get that close.'

They were both correct. I had another answer though. 'How about a sniper?' Then I inclined my head for them to both come and see the view from the window. Jermaine came too, as did Aladdin.

If I had a sniper rifle and the faintest idea how to use it, I could shoot whoever I wanted from up here. The palace grounds were swarming with security, but I suspected Prince Zebrahim would have ensured no one was assigned to check this particular tower. It was a long stretch, but it felt right. A sniper was going to take the shot from this very window, and they were probably on their way here right now. I had to move, and I had to move fast, placing all my chips on a single square and hoping I was right.

Arriving out of breath at the base of the tower, I surprised everyone there as I jumped down the last few steps with Jermaine hard on my heels.

'Where's the Maharaja?' asked Barbie, peering up the stairs to see if he was following. I carried on straight past her and to the door which I peeked out of to make sure the coast was clear.

'We missed him,' Jermaine told her. 'Not by much but they had already moved him.'

'Moved him? Moved him where?' asked Lord Edgar.

I gave him and everyone else an apologetic look as I admitted, 'Still not sure.' I had an idea though. It was horrible but if I thought like a despot desperate to run a country and do so under a regime of harsh laws, then I would be easily capable of doing what I thought they planned to do. I turned to my friends as I pushed the door open. 'We need to move. Sorry, no time to explain.' Then I went outside and held the door for everyone else to get out.

'Hold on,' Barbie said, pausing at the base of the stairs and looking up them. 'Where's Deepa and Martin?'

The Real Maharaja

I'm not really one to believe the crazy conspiracy theories you sometimes read. I was quite content to believe that JFK was killed by a lone gunman. I didn't believe that Elvis was really still alive, and I saw no reason to suspect that NASA had faked the moon landings. There was a conspiracy going on in the Maharaja's palace though and it had more moving parts than I could count.

'We have to get to the coronation,' I said once the team had followed me into a room that no one was using. 'To do that we have to go unnoticed by everyone around us.'

'How do we do that, dear lady?' asked Lord Edgar, trying the charm yet again.

'By making ourselves invisible.' I let my answer hang for a second before explaining. It seemed like a lifetime ago now, but on my second night aboard the Aurelia, I had dressed as a chef and walked about in the upper deck restaurant where there were other chefs without anyone paying me any attention. In the uniform of a servant, I had essentially been invisible. We needed to try the same trick now.

Lord Edgar didn't argue with the concept, but he didn't get how being invisible would help us. 'Explain again please; how do we find the Maharaja?'

'I think I know where he is.' From my raised viewing point at the top of the tower, once I knew what to look for, I had spotted it almost immediately. Now I just had to get there and hope I wasn't too late.

He accepted my cryptic answer with a shrug. 'Let us not dawdle then. Where do we find uniforms?'

'I can take care of that,' said Aladdin, stepping forward. 'However, I need your butler to help me, Eminence. Dressed as a guard no one will question him unless we run into more guards.'

Jermaine clapped him on the shoulder. 'Then let us pray that we do not. Time is of the essence.' Then he ducked back out the door with Aladdin, the two of them a far smaller target but he was right about time running out. The fake Maharaja was sitting on a huge throne raised above everyone else and the vizier was conducting the ceremony while everyone in the seated audience and the surrounding crowd looked on. I didn't know how long it ought to take but thought about the royal ceremonies back home in England and figured I was good for a little while yet.

Up in the tower I couldn't hear what they were saying down at the coronation, the breeze outside and the thick glass keeping the sound at bay. Down here a loudspeaker system carried the vizier's voice clearly.

Impatiently, I checked my phone: no new messages.

All around me in the small room, my friends both new and old looked pensive. I had to tell them my plan to distract them from the danger we were about to face. The door banged open, startling everyone to show just how anxious we all were. It was just Jermaine and Aladdin though, their arms full of servants' uniforms.

Rick helped to unburden Aladdin. 'That was quick.'

'Laundry is just around the corner,' explained Jermaine. 'We waited until the men in there were distracted and then grabbed all we could.'

I reached into the pile, snagging the first set of clothing my hand came to. It was a simple white tunic with gold brocade down the front and a black wrap that went around the legs with more brocade along the bottom edge. 'Everyone, grab a set and put it on.'

Huffing as he pulled his shirt off, Akamu asked, 'What are we doing, Patricia?'

'Will there be stairs?' asked Rick. 'And can I light a fire?'

I thought about that. 'Actually, I don't think a fire will help us this time.' I needed to tell them my plan though. The last twenty minutes had involved a lot of internal arguing with myself, going back and forth with different scenarios ever since I glimpsed the answer. However, I couldn't find a hole in my theory, so I had to roll the dice now and play it out. As I slipped the guard's tunic off and put my arms into the white servant's dress, I told them what I had come up with.

'We're all going to get shot,' concluded Rick when I finished.

I worried that he had a point but since we were definitely going to get shot or beheaded or something anyway, I wasn't actually gambling with anyone's life. Rather than point out the stakes, I said, 'Only if I'm wrong. I'm going. Anyone who wants to join me, I welcome.' I knew I could count on most of the people present, they had been through this with me before.

Barbie summed it up nicely though. 'It's not like we have a choice, guys. You heard those guards earlier. If we don't stop Prince Zebrahim, he'll kill us all to protect what we know.'

Thankful that I wasn't the one to manipulate the undecideds, I checked my white servant's turban was straight and went out the door.

We were in the open now. Ahead of us across the grass of the ornate garden was a marquee the size of a small village. It was to house the coronation dinner that would take place shortly after the ceremony finished. Servants dressed exactly the same as us were going back and forth with plates and boxes and other items, most of them picking them up from the back of vans parked in a small courtyard so their tyres did not ruin the immaculate lawn.

To disguise our direction, Jermaine grabbed a box and walked it most of the way to the marquee. Then he dumped it and turned right, heading for the coronation on the other side of the palace wall. There was a gate ahead of us, two armed royal guards standing just this side of it. Hideki saw them too and accelerated his pace slightly to catch up with Jermaine.

'Where do you think you're going?' asked one of the guards with a sneer as we closed the distance to them. 'Turn around and go back. No servants near the ceremony.' Then I saw his double take when he noticed that the two Zangrabarian servants were in fact a tall Jamaican and a Japanese man. He started to raise his weapon, but he was far too late to stop Jermaine punching him in his throat and stripping the gun from his hands. Hideki leapt high in the air, his right leg scything down to strike the other guard on the crown of his head. Even with the turban on, the blow was sufficient to knock the man out.

Jermaine expertly checked the weapons, then handed one to Rick and one to Akamu, the two among us most used to handling firearms. My concern that the fight might draw the attention of other guards dissipated when we came through the gate. On the other side, the audience for the coronation was facing away from us with not one person looking our way.

I promptly turned right which took me further away from the coronation but toward a pair of waiting ambulances, tucked out of the way in a parking lot a half mile away from where all the other catering vans, press vehicles with multiple antennae on top, and other emergency response vehicles were parked. With so many people congregated in one place, having emergency vehicles parked close to the main event might seem like a natural precaution. I thought I knew better though.

Ahead of me, Hideki and Jermaine approached the nearest ambulance, both glancing back for me to nod at them before they positioned themselves near the back doors. Then, poised and waiting while the rest of us got in place, they watched as Barbie silently counted down on her fingers and waved for the team to go.

This was how we discussed it just before setting off. We had the element of surprise this way and would either scare the heck out of some innocent paramedics or finally get lucky.

Rick and Akamu kept the guns out of sight and stayed close to the back doors, when Barbie's count hit zero, Lord Edgar knocked loudly on the driver's door of one ambulance and the passenger door of the other. They were parked next to each other so he could reach both doors at the same time and attract the attention of both drivers. It created a moment's distraction in which Agnes and Mavis yanked open the back doors. Then Rick and Akamu each pointed a weapon into a different ambulance, covering Jermaine, Hideki, Aladdin and Barbie as they threw themselves inside.

What I had spotted from the tower was two pairs of ambulances. Where all the other vehicles were parked, including police and fire services, I could make out one pair. And then there was this pair, sitting incongruously, half a mile from everyone else and right next to the coronation as if certain they would be needed.

As the doors opened, I knew my guess was on the money because the man standing over the patient strapped to the gurney held a gun not a stethoscope.

It just so happened that the ambulance containing the Maharaja was the one that Jermaine and Barbie went into. They were unarmed, but the element of surprise, and Jermaine's skill, guaranteed their safety. He vaulted through the door, knocked the weapon from the fake paramedic's hand and chopped at his throat with an iron fist. Something similar was happening in the other ambulance as it rocked on its suspension.

Seeing the assailant taken out, Rick moved to cover the driver, distracting him with the gun while Jermaine ducked through the partition in the front of the ambulance to subdue him. Hideki appeared to have done the same in the other ambulance before Akamu could even get there.

It had taken about four seconds.

As I stepped into the ambulance, my phone beeped in my pocket. It was the message I hoped to get and one which allowed me to breathe a very large sigh of relief. I replied before slipping the phone back into my pocket. Then I looked down to find the Maharaja strapped to the bed. Jermaine was already undoing the binds holding him down, but it was clear that the young king was drugged. The fake paramedic and the driver were being bundled into the small space between the bed and the bulkhead, Barbie binding them with gauze tape and gagging their mouths with Rick's help.

Lord Edgar's face appeared between the now closed rear doors of the ambulance as he peeked in. 'Did we get him?' he asked, his tone that of a man desperate to hear good news.

I nodded at him with a victorious smile. 'He's drugged. I need Hideki.'

Moments later the British ambassador reappeared with my Japanese friend, who I knew to be a final year med student in Japan. 'He's drugged?' Hideki asked as he swung into the back of the ambulance. It was getting a bit crowded inside, but we made way for the budding medical professional to get to the patient.

He took the king's wrist to feel his pulse, then peeled back a pupil to see his eyes. The Maharaja tried to sit up at that point, coming awake but still clearly very drugged and groggy. Hideki clasped his hand either side of the Maharaja's head to gently lower him back down. 'It's most likely an opioid,' he told us as he started rooting through drawers. 'I need Naloxone. It will be in a single use syringe but might be in a box.' He spelt the name out for us as everyone started looking for the drug.

He found it first anyway, bit the protective plastic top off and jabbed it hard into the royal's upper thigh meat. The effect was almost immediate, the Maharaja drawing in a lungful of air in a huge gasp as he sat up again. All of us moved to intercept him, our hands forming a protective barrier for him to bounce off in case he flopped to the side.

Then he smacked his lips together sleepily and stared about. It took a couple of seconds, but his eyes finally focused, and he frowned at me. He looked confused for a moment, but then, he said, 'Mrs Fisher?'

Startled that he knew who I was, I began, 'How...'

'I recognise you from your pictures,' the Maharaja answered. 'Why are you dressed as a palace servant?'

'Yay!' squealed Barbie, clapping her hands together and jumping up and down in excitement.

I smiled a smile so wide it threatened to tear my face in two. 'Welcome back, Your Majesty. It is so lovely to meet you in person. How are you feeling?'

He blinked blearily. 'A little light-headed and very confused. Where am I?'

'In an ambulance. The better question for me to answer would be: when are you? The answer to which is that you are about to miss your own coronation. There is a conspiracy to steal your crown, and I need your help to stop that from happening. Do you think you can walk?'

'Mrs Fisher. If needed, I can do acrobatics. I assume my uncle is behind this?'

'The depth of the conspiracy is still unclear, but I have a plan to blow the cover off the whole thing with your assistance.'

'Very well, Mrs Fisher. Please lead on.' Then the young king swung his legs over the side of the gurney and dropped to the floor of the ambulance.

It was time for a showdown.

Causing a Commotion

As the Maharaja exited the rear doors of the ambulance, he found Aladdin waiting for him, the valet positively vibrating with relief to see his king. The Maharaja hugged Aladdin in a genuine display of affection. He didn't pause for long though, he sensed my urgency and was right behind me as I set off for the coronation taking place ahead of us. There were a dozen of us dressed in the white and black outfit of the palace servants, six of us flanking the young Maharaja to each side where his golden robes with their deep red hues stood out like the flame atop a match.

We attracted attention, a small group of maybe half a dozen guards spotting us as we walked purposefully toward the temporary stands containing the audience. They were over by the gate where we subdued the two guards, their shouts when they recognised us filled with anger and threat as they started running in our direction with guns drawn.

The Maharaja wheeled around to face them, lifted his right arm and commanded them to stop. I saw their expressions change as they recognised their ruler, their gun arms wavering as confusion robbed their intended course of action.

With his hands placed calmly behind his back, the Maharaja addressed them, 'Gentlemen, you are right to be baffled by my presence here when you already know me to be over there.' He pointed to the coronation. 'A double has replaced me as part of a plot against this country. For the glory of Zangrabar we are going to spoil that plot and I need your muscle and tenacity to strengthen my arm. Your colleagues are in there even now, unwittingly protecting a fake Maharaja. I want no bloodshed. We cannot harm our fellow countrymen, so we must tread carefully, keep our weapons aimed down and offer no threat until it becomes necessary. Are you with me?' His final words were spoken more loudly than the rest of his speech and demanded an answer. The poor guards looked even more confused now though than before.

One was brave enough to ask a question though. 'But Your Majesty, how do we know that you are not the fake?'

The Maharaja was ready for the question though. 'You are aware that the Maharaja has a distinctive birthmark, yes?' Before they could answer, he pulled open his tunic to reveal a crescent shaped birthmark on his chest. The bright red mark looking almost exactly like a moon floating in a starless sky.

Each of the men took to one knee and bowed their heads. This was great! Now it wasn't just crazy old Patricia and her friends. Now we had some backup.

The Maharaja commanded his royal guards to rise and started back on his direct line path for the coronation. There was a gap through the centre of the raised seats so that it formed two distinct blocks with a corridor down the middle. The Maharaja walked boldly down the corridor with the rest of us following and a pair of his guards leading.

Nothing much happened when he first emerged, but the whispers started once a few more of us were visible and the sound grew quickly so that it soon drew the attention of the people at the front of the audience who turned to see what was happening.

On the stage, the fake Maharaja was sitting on his throne while the vizier directed the actions of several clerics. To his right as we looked at it, Prince Zebrahim stood a respectful distance away, watching his fake nephew be crowned.

The general was in the first row of dignitaries, mere feet from royals and heads of state from other nations. I could pick him out easily because of his hat, which was how I saw it when it turned. The general performed a perfect double take, glancing once and turning back to the stage and then whipping his head around as the news from his eyes reached his brain. He was the first to stand, a motion which drew the attention of Prince Zebrahim.

On stage, the prince stiffened, and the fake Maharaja peered out from behind the vizier, who was, at that moment, placing a golden turban on his head as part of the act of coronation.

In front of me, the Maharaja wasn't slowing down despite the growing unrest in the crowd and the cameras swinging his way as television crews mounted on raised boom arms took notice. I did my best to squash my nerves, telling myself that the worst was probably over.

On the stage, the prince didn't take long to recover his composure. His face contorted into a sneer as he raised an arm and yelled, 'Guards! Seize them!'

There must have been one hundred or more guards in attendance at the ceremony, lining the edges of the stage in ceremonial dress, guarding exits from the seating area, and dotted about here and there in small clumps for security. Most of them reacted to the prince's order but instantly hesitated when they followed his arm and saw who he was pointing at.

The Maharaja just kept on walking, never altering his pace or looking flustered. In the front row of the audience, the general moved to intercept us, not actually blocking the Maharaja's path, but getting in the way so he would have to be dealt with.

On the stage, the prince had turned purple with rage. 'I order you to seize them!' he bellowed, saliva flying from his lips as he ranted. 'He is impersonating the Maharaja!'

Finally, the Maharaja reached the front of the seats and paused. 'Sit down, General Aziz. I will get to you shortly.' He delivered the instruction in a quiet, calm tone, managing to sound regal and utterly in control despite the mayhem around him. Thus far he hadn't even bothered to acknowledge his uncle's presence, let alone the order that he be restrained.

However, as the general sheepishly retook his seat, the Maharaja turned his attention to the guards at the steps on the stage. In their ceremonial dress they looked very fancy but were no less deadly for it and the extra shiny ceremonial swords they carried were most likely still sharp enough to skewer a person. 'Step aside.'

The two directly in front of him glanced at each other and back at the young king, then did exactly as they were asked, deciding that the problem of sorting out who was who was above their pay grade.

The Maharaja placed one foot on the steps and paused, turning back to look at me and extend his hand. 'Will you come with me please, Mrs Fisher? I believe I will need your assistance for this part.'

How could I say no to that?

'What is the meaning of this?' demanded Prince Zebrahim, trying to maintain the pretence even now. 'Who are you?' He moved to the front of the stage as the Maharaja led me up the steps. Microphones on the stage were picking up every word, the decision to televise the event ensuring that millions of people were watching all around the world. Speakers mounted on the stage and around the stands amplified the sound on stage, so the vizier's voice and the details of the ceremony could be heard. The only sound they carried now though was the prince's indignant tone.

The Maharaja continued to ignore his uncle as if he was insignificant, but when we reached the top of the stairs, with two guards leading the way, he blocked our path. Unsure about how they were supposed to act, the two guards glanced at the Maharaja, who used two fingers of one hand to dismiss them to the side.

'Uncle, any further acts of treason on your part will not be well received. I need to address the nation and explain what they are seeing since this is a live event. Stand aside or I will have you restrained.'

If the prince could manage to look or be more angry, I think the top of his head would pop off. He didn't move though, instead he leaned forward to whisper, 'You're about to find out how out-matched you are.'

The Maharaja didn't know what his uncle was talking about, but I did. He had an ultimate solution which was why the Maharaja had been in the ambulance already. Like it or not, it was time for me to say something. 'Your Majesty, I believe I can shed some light on what has been happening.'

The king and the prince continued to stare at one another with the whole world watching. The prince was six inches taller and five decades older but neither factor cowed the Maharaja. He motioned to the guards that led him to the ceremony and onto the stage, calling them to him. When they stepped forward, their feet quick to obey, he kept eye contact with his uncle and said loud enough for the world to hear, 'If the prince moves... kill him.'

A thousand gasps echoed around the crowd, many more undoubtedly rippling across the globe as the world heard his instruction. The prince twitched, looking like he intended to grab the Maharaja but before I could blink there were two swords barring his way, the guards holding back from drawing blood, but making their intention clear.

Prince Zebrahim backed away, feigning a smile of acceptance and gave a small bow as he deferred to the king.

Now, with nothing stopping or distracting him, the Maharaja turned to the audience. He took a moment, glancing at me with a tight grin. Then he addressed the world. 'Citizens of Zangrabar, assembled dignitaries, royal houses and heads of state, ladies and gentlemen watching wherever you are, I apologise for the interruption to the ceremony. Unbeknownst to everyone here in Zangrabar, a plot was underway to steal the throne away from me. The young man sitting on my throne who was very nearly crowned as the new ruler of Zangrabar is, from what I understand, a very good double. I use the phrase, "As I understand," very specifically because I have been held captive for the last six days. I am here now only through the tenacity and strength of the lady to my right and her friends, who placed their very lives on the line to rescue me.' He stopped then, taking a moment to speak only to me. 'If you are ready, Mrs Fisher, I would dearly like to know what has been going on under my nose and in my absence.'

I swallowed hard. 'How many people are watching this?'

I saw the young king do some mental calculation. 'With social media and how swiftly the world is now able to react when people start sharing live feeds, I would say somewhere between one and three billion.'

A rude word arrived on my lips, but I bit it down and smiled instead. I was already on the stage and the world was waiting for me to speak. Glancing about at the cameras looking down at me, I swallowed hard again, wished there was gin and gathered my thoughts.

'Um...' I stuttered, gave myself a mental slap for being terrified and tried again. 'You are most likely wondering what connection a middle-aged, strangely dressed, English woman has to the Maharaja of Zangrabar. Hopefully, many of you will have read a story in the press a few weeks ago or seen on TV that a missing sapphire was returned here. I was the person that discovered its whereabouts and sent it back. For that service, the Maharaja graciously invited my friends and me to attend the coronation.'

'It was soon obvious to me that all was not well at the palace. I was warned that the Maharaja had been replaced, the message coming from his most loyal servant, a valet called Aladdin who had been at the Maharaja's side since birth. The double is so accurate though that few others could tell the difference. The valet had been dismissed from the Maharaja's service because they knew he would be able to reveal the conspiracy, but there were others in the palace who would be able to tell the fake Maharaja from the real one and these persons were the ones behind the conspiracy. Prince Zebrahim, the Maharaja's uncle, was one such conspirator.'

'I told you about the double,' the prince shouted. 'You would not have known about him if it were not for me. How is that a conspiracy?' He turned his gaze to the Maharaja. 'Dundegan,' he started, his voice soft as he used the Maharaja's first name, 'I did all this to protect you. I

163

discovered a plot to overthrow the crown and employed the double to ensure an assassin would kill him and not you.'

The fake Maharaja, who until now had kept quiet and tried to avoid attention by not moving, suddenly piped up. 'Assassin? I was supposed to be live bait for an assassin? You never said anything about that.'

The prince glanced across the palace grounds. It was not the first time he had done so since we arrived on stage. No one else knew what was distracting him and I don't think anyone else noticed. I did though.

The Maharaja asked his uncle a question. 'If I was being kept safe, what was I doing in the back of an ambulance and drugged?'

'It was the general!' the prince blurted, raising a finger to point at the startled soldier. 'At this very moment, he has troops waiting to storm the palace and seize control.' The general, who had been slowly sneaking along the front row to the edge, froze in the spotlight attention of cameras and faces as everyone looked where the prince was pointing. 'I couldn't move on him until I was sure of his intentions but had readied a force to repel his soldiers. You would have been safe, my king. Safe because I took control and made certain you would be out of the way when the invasion happened. The ambulance was to take you to safety, and the drugs to protect you from ever knowing how disloyal your most senior military advisor had become.'

The general had given up trying to escape, his exit was blocked by the royal guard anyway. 'It was you, Prince Zebrahim. You were the one that convinced me I needed to act for the good of the country.' Cameras whizzed about on boom arms and tripods to get a better view of his face, the prince's co-conspirator spilling the beans for all to hear. The prince looked into the distance again, staring up at the palace and looking annoyed. 'I was always loyal to the crown, but you said the Maharaja's proposed reforms were dangerous and would tear the country and region apart. You said it was down to me to ensure the future of Zangrabar by backing you.'

Again the prince glanced at the palace.

'What is it you are looking for, Prince Zebrahim?' asked the Maharaja.

'His sniper,' I replied though the question hadn't been aimed at me. 'Isn't that right, Prince?' The prince gave a little head shake of denial, looking around for anyone that might help him. 'That is why you were in the ambulance, Your Majesty. The prince intended to have the fake Maharaja shot.'

'What?' the fake Maharaja snapped, sitting forward in his chair and then ducking out of it to hide behind the throne.

'Most likely a head shot because it guarantees fatality and makes it harder to identify the body accurately. To be sure though, the ambulance was manned with men loyal to your uncle. You would have been shot in the head as soon as the assassination took place so that the time of death would match. The fake Maharaja's body would be carried to the ambulance which was parked nearby to ensure it got here first, and then discarded so the body taken to the morgue would be identified as yours. Your birthmark is the one thing the double couldn't fake.'

'Then, using the assassination as a signal, the general's troops would swoop on the palace, giving the prince a legitimate and obvious person to blame for the assassination. You would be dead, he would be hailed as a hero for defeating the attempted coup and would then be crowned as the new Maharaja.'

'This is all nonsense,' railed the prince. 'There is no sniper. If what you say were true, he would surely have shot the Maharaja the moment he appeared.'

I raised my hand and made a gun shape with it. Then pointed at the floor by the prince's feet.

A neat hole appeared in the floor two inches from his right foot, followed quickly by the crack and echo of the shot coming from the north tower. Screams and cries of anguish filled the air. I knew it was a risky thing to do, so as pandemonium broke out and secret service agents from three dozen countries all tried to get their principles to cover, I called for calm. 'Sorry! Sorry, that wasn't cool. There is no danger to anyone. I needed to prove a point though. The sniper is currently in the custody of two very good friends of mine; one of whom just fired that shot.'

The gaggle of royal guards in the process of diving at the Maharaja to protect him with their bodies, backed away again as he thanked them and waved them off. 'Is there anything further, Mrs Fisher?'

I bit my lip. 'Actually, there is. Beyond your valet, Aladdin, there were three people who could easily identify the fake. Each of them needed to be complicit in the conspiracy for it to hold. The general was, of course, too dumb to realise he was being lied to and led to his death by the mastermind behind the Maharaja's assassination, the prince, but he needed a third person to play along.'

'You are referring of course to me,' said the vizier. He looked far too calm for a man accused of treason. 'I was complicit, but only in the element that the prince revealed to me. I believed his story about protecting the Maharaja by using a sacrificial double. I went along with it because I am loyal to the throne and he convinced me I would be doing the Maharaja a service by preventing his death.' He smiled broadly at the Maharaja. 'I am, and have always been, your true servant.'

'Why did you put the snake in my room?' He snapped his eyes back in my direction, looking worried and baffled at the same time, no doubt wondering how on earth I could know it was him behind the attempts on my life. 'When the prince came to me last night, he was genuinely surprised that I had been attacked because he knew nothing about it. He didn't like me sticking my nose in, but he was too arrogant to believe I could work out what was happening in time or probably ever.'

The vizier wasn't ready to admit his guilt yet though. 'Why would you think the snake was anything to do with me? You have no evidence, Mrs Fisher. I am loyal to the crown.'

'You were seen by two of my friends. That was why you had them taken away and medically inebriated. I assume they wouldn't have lived to receive their public flogging, conveniently getting killed in a jailhouse brawl or some such other terrible and unfortunate tragedy they would have brought on themselves.' I watched the vizier's face for signs that I was about right but he didn't need to tip me off for the charges to stick. 'The part you don't know yet is that they escaped.' Now his eyes bugged out. 'I have friends with... unusual skills.'

Rick chose that moment to shout his displeasure. 'Honestly, in a country with no alcohol, you get me drunk anyway but I don't get to taste a drop. That's just plain cruel, man.' Dozens of cameras had swung to focus on his face, but he had nothing further to add.

I continued. 'The two men you sent to jail just helped to rescue the Maharaja and will be quite happy to identify you as the man they saw carrying a large snake along the secret passageway behind our rooms. When that failed, you sent a cleric dressed as a guard to kill me. Only then did the prince realise what was going on and demand that you desist. I asked too many questions, didn't I? That was why you decided to get rid of me. I was already famed for solving the mystery of the missing sapphire and there I was asking questions when you were just about to kill the Maharaja. What did the prince promise you? Or was it sufficient that you would eliminate a king who planned to give rights to women, to employ modern medical practices to reduce infant mortality and to challenge the ancient religious practices you promote?'

The vizier's face was a mask of anger, his role as a man of peace long forgotten as he clenched his fist. 'You stupid interfering woman! How could you possibly understand the needs of this country?' Then he charged, rabid spittle flying from his mouth as he slipped away from the guards standing behind him and ran at me. He cried, 'Arrrrrgh!' at the top of his lungs, raising his staff to strike me and I thought nothing was going to stop him until a puff of red exploded from his right shoulder and he spun away from the impact. He had forgotten about the sniper in the north tower and as he crashed to the ground the chasing guards bundled on top of him.

My legs felt weak. It was done. I had solved the riddle of the fake Maharaja, and everyone I came with was still alive as was the real Maharaja who was now safe to be crowned and rule his country. The last forty something hours had been filled with horror and danger and threat, but it was over, and I could finally stop.

As I considered that and what I would do next, I realised how much I wanted a gin and tonic. Not that I could have one until I got back on the plane and out of Zangrabar airspace, of course. I was still on the stage with the guards and the Maharaja, only vaguely aware of my surroundings or what my eyes were looking at, I felt exhausted and elated and ready to sit somewhere quiet for a while.

Then the sound of clapping and cheering reached my ears. It was getting louder as more people joined in. The Maharaja was standing at the front of the stage but my initial assumption that they were cheering their new king faded as I saw him egg them on.

They were cheering for me.

A lump formed in my throat when the Maharaja beckoned me to join him at the edge of the stage. The world was watching and what they could see was me. Wearing a servant's outfit with unkempt hair poking out from an ill-fitting turban and still plastered in harem makeup because there hadn't been time to wipe it off properly. None of that mattered though because people were cheering for me. I could make out echoes of my name being chanted.

'Zangrabar!' the Maharaja roared. 'I give you the twice saviour of our nation, Patricia Fisher. Forever more today will be a Zangrabar national holiday known as Fisher's Day. It will be the day preceding the anniversary of my coronation which will take place tomorrow.' Then he chuckled. 'Once I have found time to appoint a new vizier.'

The crowd laughed with him and he let go my hand so he could step away from me to join in their applause. It was overwhelming, a tear escaping my right eye as I tried hard to hold it together. It was too much for me but then I couldn't take all the credit; there had been a whole team of us involved. In front of the stage, the royal guards were doing a good job of keeping the crowd under control, not least to spare the dignitaries and VIPs in the front row. My friends were down there somewhere though, and I waved frantically for them to join me when I spotted them.

It took a moment, but the guards got the message and let them through. Jermaine leading Lord Edgar with Barbie and Hideki behind, then

Rick and Akamu with Agnes and Mavis and finally Aladdin. 'Wait,' I said, 'there's two more.' Martin Baker and Deepa Bhukari were making their way through the crowd being escorted by a large contingent of the royal guard. I would discover later that it had been Deepa that fired both shots from the sniper rifle, her skill with a gun honed during a previous career in the Pakistani military. They joined the others and each of them were welcomed onto the stage by the young Maharaja, personally shaking hands with everyone, asking their names and then announcing them to the world.

He had to pause briefly because Barbie had spotted the fake Maharaja still hiding behind his throne and, together with Deepa, they were giving him some unfriendly advice regarding his attitude toward women.

When the girls were done and my friends were all formed up on stage, they looked just as bewildered by the attention as I felt. I started clapping along with everyone else and decided it was time to step out of the spotlight. Taking a step back, my foot caught on a cable at the edge of the stage and in true Patricia fashion, I tripped, slipped, wobbled, used my arms to get my balance, overcorrected, and fell off the stage.

On my way to the ground, I knew the one thing the world would remember above everything else was me landing on my head and showing my knickers to the world.

I slept late the next day, the option of getting up early for fitness dismissed without a second thought. When finally I did claw my way out of bed, the sun was high in the sky and the hastily rejigged coronation was no more than a few hours away.

This time I was going to attend it. The silliness of the red carpet, and all the pretence Prince Zebrahim had employed to drive the general and the vizier to their extreme ends, was gone. In its place would be a dignified and respectful ceremony conducted by the new vizier.

There was nothing for me to do except relax, turn up, enjoy the spectacle and attend the banquet afterwards. That sounded manageable but we needed to leave as the sun was setting because we were due to meet the Aurelia in Egypt the following morning. The Maharaja extended an invitation to stay as long as we wanted, and I think it was an offer that would last my lifetime if I so desired. I wanted to get back to the ship though. Even though all the excitement here was over, and I could enjoy the beauty of the nation, I was restless to return to Alistair, a man I felt great affection for.

I had time to kill before the coronation and nothing to do with it, so I snuggled into a chair, tucked my legs under my bottom, plopped Anna on my lap, and read a book. Yesterday, I found Anna exactly where I expected to; in the room down the passageway where the Corgis were staying. She trotted happily out to me when the very British butler there answered the door, looking pleased with herself. The contented glow of satisfaction radiated out from her even now as she snuggled into me. The book, a novel about a woman on a ship getting embroiled in murder and mystery was just silly and fantastical. I packed it with a plan to read it during my quiet times on this trip but had not yet had the chance to read the first page. I soon lost myself in it and was startled when a knock came at the door.

Anna burst into life, going from snoring and fully asleep to a tiny toothed weapon of destruction in half a second as she leapt from my lap to run at the door; she wasn't so satisfied with life that people could dare to knock at the door without dying for their crime.

Jermaine, once again insisting that I not be let out of his sight in case something happened to me, appeared from an alcove and walked slowly toward the front entrance. He disappeared into the small lobby area, scooped my still barking dog, and was illuminated by a shaft of light as he opened the door.

Moments later he returned with a troop of royal guards following him and the Maharaja, who was able to get about using his own feet and didn't need to be taken everywhere on a bed of cushions.

I got to my feet the moment I saw him, bowing my head and wishing I had put clothes on and wasn't still slobbing about in my pyjamas. 'Your Majesty, I was not expecting company.'

He waved a dismissal with one hand. 'Please, Mrs Fisher. It is I who have intruded on you. Please accept my apologies for arriving unannounced. Since you are leaving today, and I can expect to be in high demand from the coronation onwards, I wanted to take a few minutes to thank you in person.'

'You already did that, Your Majesty.'

'I thanked you publicly, now I can thank you privately. My country owes you and your friends a great debt of gratitude. There is no way that we can ever repay it, but we will always honour you.'

'I did only that which was necessary. You are most generous and kind.'

'And you, Mrs Fisher, are the most modest person I have ever met.'

There were things I wanted to ask for my own closure. I wasn't sure they were the sort of questions I would get answers to, but I gave it a go anyway. 'Your Majesty, what is to become of your double?' To my mind the teenage boy was guilty but ought not to be held accountable for his actions too stringently. That was not my decision to make though and having asked the question, I now worried I might hear that his hands had been cut off in punishment.

The Maharaja's reply placed my mind at ease though, 'He is on one of my private jets being returned to America with his family.'

'They were here?'

'A mother and a younger sister. They were staying in another of the staterooms, my uncle having made all the arrangements.'

'How did he find him?' I asked, thoroughly curious about how a prince in Zangrabar had managed to find a double for his nephew in America.

'He put out an advertisement in a paper. It called for child actors that resembled the picture it showed. The picture, of course, was me. It gave height and weight and accent required.'

'I think he got lucky to find someone so similar. So, you just sent them home?'

'It gave me a reason to contact the US Foreign Secretary. I intend to re-establish our connection and have them open an embassy here next year.' The young king gave me a knowing look. 'You also wish to ask about the vizier, the general and my uncle, yes?' I thought about saying no but it would have been a lie. I didn't need to say anything though because he was already talking. 'They remain in custody awaiting trial. I am fairly sure they will be found guilty but where Zangrabarian law calls for them to be executed by being boiled in vinegar, I intend to repeal the law. They may deserve it, but this nation deserves a better future in which punishment for crimes involves an opportunity for rehabilitation. General Aziz provided a full confession. In it he admits to sending the fighter aircraft that tried to shoot you down. Like the vizier, he feared you would ask too many questions when they were so close to achieving their goal. Had the three of them worked together, I imagine they would have been unstoppable.'

To change the subject, I said, 'At least now I know what mystery it was that you alluded to in your telegram.'

The Maharaja's brow creased. 'Really? How so?'

Now I was baffled. 'Surely you were referring to the odd behaviour of your uncle and the vizier as they plotted against you.'

He chuckled. 'Goodness no. I had no idea they were up to anything until the moment I was lured into the north tower and trapped in there.'

'So what was it then?' I asked sitting forward with curiosity.

'My mother's cookbook went missing. She died many years ago as you know but she liked to cook even though she was the wife of a Maharaja. I have kept her hand-written recipe book ever since she passed but now I cannot find it and I had hoped you might turn your sleuthing skills to find it for me. It is no matter now.'

I thought about that for a moment, then got to my feet. 'Can you give me just a minute to get dressed, Your Majesty? I think I know where it will be.' He opened his mouth in surprise but closed it again and swept his hand in a gesture that told me to take my time.

174

Just a few minutes later, I was dressed enough to be seen in public and heading back out the door next to the Maharaja. Anna tugged my right arm with her lead and seemed propelled by her tail as it wagged furiously back and forth. Wherever we were going, she wanted to get there first. Her antics amused the Maharaja, but what he asked was, 'Where are we going, Mrs Fisher?'

'To the harem,' I replied.

To my surprise the young man's cheeks coloured. 'My father's sex slaves. It was the one thing he and I argued about more than anything,' he reminisced. 'They are still here, I believe, but I have already abolished the practice.'

'I thought the girls there were all volunteers.'

'And well compensated too. It is hardly a modern, forward-thinking practice though. If I intend to steer this country towards sexual equality, among other things, I can hardly promote careers for women and tell the next generation they can be lawyers or doctors while actively paying for prostitutes.' I felt like congratulating the young man. He was wise beyond his years and able to see past the raging hormones that dominate the thoughts of every other sixteen-year-old boy I have ever met. I didn't say any of that though, too worried I would come across as condescending.

We walked the rest of the way in silence, arriving a few minutes later. I knocked on the door, but this time found that it just opened. Inside, Bethansa sported a bruise to her face, her penalty for resisting the guard and clerics in pursuit of us yesterday. She bowed low to the Maharaja and rose when he commanded.

'Can you take me back to the room I was in yesterday?' I asked her.

'Of course,' she replied. Promptly turning around to lead me.

As the Maharaja followed me, he looked this way and that. 'I was always curious about what this place looked like. Now I know,' he said with a small shrug.

'What will happen to the ladies that lived here?' I wanted to know.

'They will all be suitably compensated and offered education and training so they may pursue alternative careers. It seems the least that I can do.'

The harem already had a completely different feel to it and when we arrived back in the large room they were all gathered in yesterday, many of them were there again, but had on actual clothes. Several even wore jeans, doubtless gifts from wealthy visitors from the west.

They all leapt to their feet as the Maharaja came in though he waved for them to sit again. It hadn't meant anything yesterday and barely registered at all, but when he asked about a handwritten book, I remembered seeing one in the hands of one of the ladies yesterday. On a small bookshelf in the corner of the room, several dog-eared paperbacks sat in a single row next to a pile of magazines. Hidden right at the end was a hand-written book with an aged look to it and lots of splots on the cover where soup or sauce or something had spat.

The Maharaja shook his head as I handed it to him. 'Mrs Fisher, there is no end to your ability to surprise.'

An Unexpected Loss

The coronation ceremony was a success, the new vizier and his clerics performing as if they had been practicing for weeks not hours. I left Anna in her room, it seemed the safer option as it eliminated the risk of her causing a commotion for global television or of barking loudly during an important part of the ceremony.

I sat in the front row, with my friends around me and Lord Edgar to my immediate right. His wife and children were several rows back, I knew this because the one time I glanced in that direction, I found his spouse boring holes into the back of my head with her eyes. I really wanted to tell her what a cad her husband was, but I had enjoyed enough drama for one trip.

The rest of the front row, on both sides of the central gap between the banks of seats, was taken up once again by heads of state, various global VIPs and members of other royal families. I mention the royal families because a certain Corgi-loving monarch in her nineties was sitting five seats along from me and had caught my eyes as she was led to her seat. She gave me a wink when I looked at her, which, let me tell you, is the sort of thing that stays with a person.

It was not a short ceremony, but it was filled with pomp and pageantry, the spectacle of it a joy to behold. As the Maharaja predicted, he was inundated with official tasks at the private banquet that followed, and I knew I would not get to speak with him again this day. Checking my watch revealed that it was almost time to go.

'Are you ready, madam?' asked Jermaine. The banquet hall had been divided into a central tier for the Maharaja and his honoured guests and then so many large round tables spread out across the marquee that I lost count trying to work out how many people were being catered for. It was a bit like being at a wedding. I was sitting at one such table along with all my friends, so they all heard Jermaine's enquiry.

'I am,' replied Barbie. 'Today has been incredible but getting back to normality would be nice. The food here is too rich for me as well. I feel like I have put on so much weight since we arrived.'

Jermaine raised one eyebrow. 'Oh yeah, tubby. You're really bulking up over there.' She pursed her lips at him and squinted her eyes.

'We are staying,' announced Akamu quietly. A ripple of surprise came from everyone at the table. I half expected he and Rick to do something unexpected though.

Rick gave me a tight-lipped smile of apology. 'The girls are wanted in half the countries on the planet, but they are heroes here and can live in luxury if they choose to stay.'

'Which we do,' added Mavis. Her hand was in Akamu's when she said, 'It's time to stop running and have a life.'

I was sad to say goodbye to my friends, but I always knew the day had to come. We were on a cruise after all so no matter how dearly we loved each other, there was always going to be a parting at some point.

There being nothing else to say and the window of opportunity to get to the Aurelia before it sailed again dwindling, we all stood and hugged and said our goodbyes. I had a tear in my eye as I held Rick and then Akamu, but it didn't stay there, it called for some friends and together they ran down my face to ruin my makeup and make me look ridiculous.

Barbie helped me wipe them away as she too shed a few of her own. Then we slipped quietly from the marquee, sneaking out in twos and threes so no one would see us all departing at once and be tempted to make a fuss.

The flight to Egypt to meet the Aurelia was uneventful. Unless one decides to count being united with two badly missed friends, gin and tonic. If you count that, then it was quite eventful indeed.

The End

Author Note:

There are things that each of us hopes for in life. I suspect my dreams are more modest than most. A decade ago, I was getting ready to leave the army. It was something I always knew would come so had studied and worked and thought about what I would do afterwards. At the time, I could only think about finding a better paid job and bringing in some real cashola.

Corporate life at the high end is not for the faint hearted though. I was far happier sleeping in a wet hole in the ground and getting shot at. At least there I was able to shoot back. I quit my stressful, awful job very recently and have embarked on a career as a writer with the belief that I can make enough money from it to support my wife and child. Currently, I am not doing that, and we are making changes to curtail expenditure while I feverishly force the stories in my head into words on the page.

This is no appeal for sympathy though, please don't imagine for one moment that I am not the happiest I have been in many years. I am getting up early and going to bed late because I absolutely love what I am doing. I would like to make more money from it but, honestly, I need to pay the bills and feed everyone and if there is a tenner left over to buy a couple of beers then hooray. Like I said, I have small dreams.

This week I get to take my four-year-old to forest club. Together, he and I will track animals, build shelters and learn about nature. Who can do that on a Wednesday morning when they have a full-time job in an office? I will attend his nativity this year without having to sneak out of my job and I get to have lunch with my wife every day. I undoubtedly work more hours than before, but not one of them feels like work.

So why am I telling you this? I'm just a regular guy, but one with a head full of stories. The biggest story in there is about learning to be content, a skill I learned from my father. I want for very little because I wake up each morning next to a woman I adore, and I have a son who wants nothing more than to play with his dad and help him do jobs in the house and garden.

My life is good. I hope yours is too and that you find ways to enrich it for yourself and for those around you.

On the next few pages you will find an extract from the next book, **A Sleuth and her Dachshund in Athens**. It is Patricia's eighth outing and as we draw close to the end of her cruise, I find myself being constantly asked what will happen afterwards. The annoyingly cryptic answer is that you will have to wait to find out, but it will not be nothing. I think a good series is one that has a beginning and an end though, the author finishing the story off to give the readers satisfactory closure. That is what I will give you for Patricia. For this series at least.

This is not my first series though; there are many other books already waiting for you. So, if you enjoy Patricia's adventures, you may wish to check out **Tempest Michaels**, **Amanda Harper** and **Jane Butterworth**. Like Patricia, they solve mysteries and their stories are written to make you laugh and keep you turning pages when you really ought to be going to sleep.

Finally, there is a **Patricia Fisher** story that you may not yet have found. It is part of this series but sits apart from it. It is called *Killer Cocktail* and you can have it for free. Just click the link below and tell me where to send it.

Yes! Send me my FREE Patricia Fisher story!

The Missing Sapphire of Zangrabar
The Kidnapped Bride
The Director's Cut
The Couple in Cabin 2124
Doctor Death
Murder on the Dancefloor
Mission for the Maharaja
A Sleuth and her Dachshund in Athens
The Maltese Parrot
No Place Like Home

Dead Relative

'He's dead.'

It was a simple statement, but it encapsulated everything I needed to know very quickly. I had only met him two days ago, but he was a delightful young man with a promising future. That future had been snatched away now, apparently by his own hand.

My name is Patricia Fisher. I'm just a lady on a cruise ship, but it just happens to be the Aurelia, the world's largest and most luxurious cruise liner and by the hand of fate, I am staying in the biggest and best suite it has. I'm also dating the captain of the ship, Alistair Huntley, and I have an unwelcome habit of finding dead bodies or uncovering crimes when I would rather be sitting on a sun bed reading a trashy novel and sipping gin.

The body sitting in a desk chair with his head lying next to a computer keyboard had been found after he failed to report for work this morning. Another member of crew sent to rouse him, called for security when he got no answer and that was when they discovered his body. A trickle of blood ran from his left temple to pool on the desk and a small handgun lay discarded on the floor where it had fallen from his limp hand.

The official announcement of death was made my Dr Kim, one of the ship's doctors though I thought it quite obvious from his pallor that life had left the poor young man some hours ago. As Dr Kim stepped back, his task now complete, Lieutenant Martin Baker stepped into the now vacant spot next to the body. Crew cabins were small, especially for junior personnel. Julian Young was a bursar's assistant, which in layman's terms meant he was an accountant. I knew all this already because he was also the captain's nephew, his younger sister's eldest child and someone he had proudly introduced me to when I returned to the ship from Zangrabar. I think Alistair had been happy that someone else in the family wanted to follow his path. I wondered what he would think now.

Lieutenant Baker reached over the body to click the mouse which was still gripped in Julian's hand. The screen of the computer flicked to life, displaying a word document.

Lieutenant Deepa Bhukari moved to join her colleague in reading it, curiosity getting the better of me and Dr Kim as well.

Dear Everyone,

I can no longer live with the crushing depression I suffer each day as a result of my disability. I'm sorry for the mess I leave behind for others to clear up. This is the best thing for me and for those around me. Please tell my mother that I love her.

Julian

It was a sad note and very short. It also told me that he had been murdered.

'What was his disability?' asked Deepa standing back to get some room after crowding around the screen with the rest of us. She was looking at the dead man as if trying to spot a physical abnormality.

'He was deaf,' I replied, 'He didn't see it as a disability at all which makes the authenticity of the suicide note questionable. I also know that he was right-handed.'

Both members of the security team looked at the body. 'But he shot himself with his left hand,' observed Barker, sensing what that might mean. 'This wasn't a suicide, was it?'

I pursed my lips and blew out my cheeks before I let myself make a bold statement. After a second of deliberation, I said, 'I don't think so. I met him a few hours after we got back from Zangrabar. He was pleasant to speak with and excited to meet me. He was also very excited to have a job on board his uncle's ship and couldn't stop listing all the places he was going to get to visit and all the things he was going to do. He lipread and was able to hold a conversation without the deafness being noticeable. He came on board as we got off in India, so what's that... six days? In six days, he went from happy and excited to depressed and suicidal? No, he managed to attract the attention of someone who felt the need to kill him. He was murdered, and we are going to work out who did it.'

'There's something we have to do first,' Lieutenant Baker said quietly.

'What's that?'

He sniffed deeply, the air escaping again as a sigh. 'We have to tell the captain his nephew is dead.'

A New Mystery to Solve

Alistair took the news quietly. He could tell something was wrong when he saw our faces approaching across the bridge but waited until we were alone in his private quarters before he asked Lieutenant Baker to spit it out.

He didn't argue or try to deny what he was being told. Instead, he turned around to look out the window of his cabin and stare at the endless grey ocean outside. 'Please leave me,' he said quietly. As his two officers made their way to the door, I hesitated and he turned to look at me, a single tear in his right eye. 'Please stay,' he begged as he lifted an arm in welcome. I stepped into his embrace and held him for a while.

With his heart beating against me and his chin resting on top of my head, he asked, 'Can you find the person responsible please, Patricia?'

I expected nothing less. 'Of course.' Suddenly I had a new mystery to solve; one with a personal element to it. Someone had killed Julian and I knew the full company of the ship's security team would be at my disposal in my bid to find out who and why.

We said nothing else for several minutes, both of us taking comfort in the presence and warmth of the other. Eventually though, he moved, breaking the embrace and taking a step back. 'I must return to my duties. There is much to do before we dock tonight.'

I placed a steadying hand on his arm. 'It's okay to take some time for yourself,' I told him. 'Your crew know their tasks and will make you proud.'

He nodded curtly. 'I know. However, I think it best if I keep myself busy. I don't want to dwell, and I have to work out what I am going to say when I phone my sister and her husband.'

He was probably right about distracting himself. I could only imagine how he felt right now. Julian got the job because of Alistair who admitted he had to create a post for him to occupy. He would blame himself, that much I was sure of, so now I had to prove why that was not the case.

We kissed before I left, a peck on the lips because we are lovers and then I left him to gather himself. Outside, I found Baker and Bhukari waiting for me in the passageway. The captain's private quarters are situated behind the bridge, high up in the superstructure to give a commanding view of the ship and to place him immediately to hand when an emergency occurred during his off-duty periods. Normally, only crew ever got to come up to the bridge, but our relationship had bent the rules a little so that I now had my own access pass to the crew only elevator.

On the walk back to the elevator, both officers followed me. 'Where do you want to start?' asked Deepa.

'Breakfast,' I replied. 'I want to start with breakfast.' I was out for my morning jog when I saw Dr Kim hurrying with his medical bag. I knew the look on his face, so I followed him which was how I came to be there when the good doctor announced Julian's death. Whatever I had planned for today was out the window now because I had a case to crack. Breakfast was necessary though, that and a shower.

My butler Jermaine was waiting for me when I got back to my suite. I had been gone for more than an hour, far longer than usual which explained the concerned look on his face. Anna, my miniature Dachshund, barked and ran across the carpet to greet me and voice her disapproval at the two people following me in. She held back from ravaging their ankles though. Her change in aggression level was partly due to some training I performed with her and partly due to being pregnant. At least I thought she was pregnant. She found her way into a pack of Corgis in Zangrabar and had mellowed since the experience.

187

Jermaine crossed the suite to take hats from the two security officers. 'Good morning, Lieutenant Bhukari, good morning, Lieutenant Baker. Is everything alright, madam?' he asked as he placed their items neatly on a shelf by the main entrance.

'Um, well... yes and no,' I relied cryptically. 'We have a mystery to look into, I'm afraid. I'll leave Deepa and Martin to fill you in on the details while I get clean and dress for the day. Is there coffee?'

'Of course, madam. What may I serve you for breakfast this morning?'

'Do we have any English muffins?'

'Of course, madam. I collected them this morning while you were out. It gave me a chance to exercise Anna.'

My stomach growled hungrily at the thought. 'Then eggs Benedict, please with a side of bacon.' Baker made a small sound of interest, his mouth almost drooling when I looked. I laughed at him. 'I'm sure we have enough for everyone if you are hungry.'

Twenty minutes later, three of us were tucking into the breakfast feast, lashings of buttery Hollandaise sauce dripping down my fork where it threatened to make my hand greasy. 'Exquisite as always, Jermaine. Thank you,' I praised him as I mopped up the last piece of egg. 'Now, I fear, we must get on with our day.' Breakfast conversation had focused on Julian Young and what might have befallen him. It was too early for conjecture, but we made a list of persons to speak with and questions to ask.

Washing down the last morsels with a glass of freshly squeezed orange juice, I dabbed my mouth with a napkin and pushed back my chair. Should I take Anna with me or leave her here? She was asleep on a couch looking quite content, so I decided to leave her behind. She didn't need the exercise and might be growing puppies in their somewhere.

'Ready when you are,' I said to Deepa and Martin. Their breakfast plates were also devoid of food, both of them putting away Jermaine's creation as if famished. They were ready though and steadfastly determined to assist me in bringing the killer to justice. Despite the suicide note and well-arranged scene, I was convinced it was murder, there were too many incongruities for it to be anything else.

The question then was; why kill him? Someone had to gain from his death and now I had to find the trail of breadcrumbs that would tell me who that was and what it was that they gained. We were at ground zero though; at this point in time I knew nothing at all and had a metaphorical mountain to climb while blindfolded.

Good: I like a challenge.

That's the end of this two-chapter teaser I'm afraid. To get your copy of the next book in this series, just click this link:

A Sleuth and her Dachshund in Athens

Made in United States
North Haven, CT
26 March 2024

50533603R00117